The Ghost in the Dunes

A Lamentation's End Novella

By Wade Lewellyn-Hughes

The Ghost in the Dunes copyright © 2020 Wade Lewellyn
All Rights Reserved
The Lamentation's End Series copyright © 2020 Wade Lewellyn
All Rights Reserved
Published by Wisdom, Wonder, & Whimsy Books
Bozeman, Montana
ISBN-13: 978-0-9908175-9-8

Edited by Inspired Ink Editing
Front cover illustrated by Andrew Ryan

Published by Wisdom, Wonder, & Whimsy Books

WWWBOOKS
Wisdom, wonder, & whimsy books

DEDICATION
For those who speak up. Black lives matter.

Contents

Central Anzante

Kruispad

The satyr ruins

Chapter I: The Slave Pits

Gbad'Wu shifted on her feet, watching Gbad'Apiyo's slim fingers work to unlock the grate over their slave pit with the keys he had stolen off the guard. In her fourteen years, the Gbad tribe had let few things deter them. But now, they were separated, tired, stripped to their smallclothes, and starving. Wu shivered and leaned into her father's embrace when the hopeless wailing in another pit started up again.

Apiyo's persistence earned him a clunk. He grinned down at them from Gbad'Tse's shoulders and worked the lock free of the grate. His younger twin brother hefted him higher to squeeze out under the heavy iron.

"Wole," Tse said, offering Gbad'Wu's father a hand up.

Almost exactly between the two brothers physically, her father still excelled as their best hunter and their best barterer. Many of the women in Anzante believed him handsome. Wu found his attempts at charm far more

1

laughable than his humor.

Once on top, her father helped Apiyo lift the grate and lay it back on its hinges.

Offering his hand and his height again, Tse hoisted Gbad'Ekon up to the others. Her long arms had no trouble reaching them.

Then it was Wu's turn. She stood on his shoulders and grabbed her father's hands. With his tug, she was free of the pit. But the desolate room of broken amphorae and the stench of waste nurtured little hope. "Maman?" she whispered to her father.

He nodded and said, "In a moment, we will find her." Then he bent to help thin Apiyo lift his muscular brother.

Her mother and Gbad'Zoya had been taken that morning. They hadn't seen the rest of the tribe since yesterday. Poor Gbad'Turu was still sick.

"Ekon?" Gbad'Wu murmured as she approached her friend staring up through a hole in the ceiling of the old satyr ruins. The stars shone brightly over the desert.

"We can reach that," Ekon said. Her pretty smile felt out of place here.

Gbad'Wu turned away from it. She wasn't interested in leaving, not without the others.

After the men helped Tse out of the pit, Ekon clicked her tongue to get their attention. She pointed up. Tse aided her height. After a peek, Ekon stood tall on his shoulders and scanned about. She ducked down and whispered, "It is empty."

"Bon," Gbad'Wu's father said. "Take Wu and hide."

"Hide?" Wu asked. "I want to help you find Maman."

"No." The tightening of his features said that was the end of it. "This Ghost is a magus. That is no fight for you." He kissed her on the forehead, then said to Tse, "Help her up."

Gbad'Ekon climbed out fully and continued to watch her surroundings.

She shook her hand in opening for Wu to grab. "Come, Wu. I see where we can hide and wait."

Small for her age, Gbad'Wu rose easily in Tse's strong arms. She ignored Ekon's hand and gripped the thick, sandy stones of the ancient marketplace to pull herself up.

She and Ekon squatted by the hole near a temple devoted to the old god Maris. Someone had desecrated the giant marble idol within, breaking off her arms and head. Domed dwellings dotted the satyr ruins in each direction. Firelight brightened the eastern end, where drumbeats and cheering echoed off the surrounding dunes. "The Ghost must be there," Wu said.

"Ekon," Gbad'Wu's father said from below. "Take her to Kruispad. Northeast. Wait for us there."

While Gbad'Ekon studied the stars, Wu threw her father an irritated expression.

His features softened before his brown eyes glistened with tears. "Allez! Be free, my daughter. We will find you there." He formed a fist and tapped it twice against his bare chest.

Spying out of the room into the oil-lamp-lit corridor between pit chambers, Apiyo leaned forward. He jerked away, put his back to the wall, and clicked his tongue. His brother and Wu's father silently moved to the side of the arched entry as Wu and Ekon bent down helplessly to watch hand in hand. Unarmed, all they could do was disarm and subdue the guards quickly.

"Another?" a guard asked, venturing closer. "He has taken four. When do we get one to play with?" The guard froze in the entry.

They had forgotten to lay the gate back over the pit. When the guard drew his scimitar, the men leaped out.

Ekon squeezed Wu's hand.

A slash caught Apiyo in the face before Tse grabbed the man's arm.

Then the second guard struck from the corridor, removing Tse's grip in a spray of blood.

Growling, Wu's father lunged. A scimitar's point pierced through his back.

"Papan!" Gbad'Wu screamed.

The guards locked eyes with her.

Ekon jerked Wu to her feet and got her running while the guards shouted below. "Northeast," she said through her tears. "Northeast, Wu. We'll be safe there."

Chapter 2: Ekons' Sacrifice

Wu stood at the top of the slope edging the olive grove and admired the pink and purple light coloring the dunes beyond the river's shelter. She glanced southwest for a moment and again tried to forget the events of that night two years ago. Dusk spread its colors over the mud-bricked buildings of Kruispad as well. Already drumbeats summoned the rarely woken festive spirits in the old city's walls. Rare as a thunderstorm this deep in southern Anzante, a night of merriment awaited her.

She adjusted the heft of the knotted wooden staff across her shoulders, weighed down by two reed baskets brimming with freshly picked olives. Carefully, she set her sandaled foot at an angle and began her descent down the steeply sloped shortcut to the packed-dirt path to Kruispad.

Something smacked the back of her head. She tumbled forward, losing control of her load. Olives peppered the rocky ground about her as she rolled to the base of the hill. Her arms scraped, her head throbbing, Wu rubbed the ache beneath her black curls. It stung, but her brown hand came away dry.

Two of Najih's darker-skinned wards slid down the slope after her.

She recognized Rouzbeh and scrabbled back. In her excitement to end the day, she had dropped her guard. Now her turn had come.

Though he received the same treatment as the other orphans conscripted into Najih's estate, Rouzbeh was the man's actual son. Wu could tell by the way his thick bottom lip hung open every time he thought too hard. Not that his blood mattered. The danger he posed presented itself in his dark eyes, possessing the same hatred for her kind as his father's did.

He sucked his lip in and pointed his long arm to his right.

The same age as Wu, a few years younger than Rouzbeh, Kahlil eyed her with a mixed expression, clearly relieved not to have been involved with her murder, though not relieved enough to drop the sharp rock from his hand. Like an obedient cur, Kahlil moved opposite Rouzbeh to block the road and Wu's escape.

"Are you ready to see your dead parents, little mute?" Rouzbeh asked. He picked up a pitted stone and tossed it in his hand.

With her gaze stuck to Rouzbeh's stone, Wu searched behind her for her pole.

"May Mulgrum crush all invaders under his mighty golden shoe!" Rouzbeh drew back his arm.

Her fingers found a basket. She jerked it forward, dumping more olives. The stone cracked the woven reeds. Wu seized the end of her pole and pulled it free of the baskets as she rose, stilling Kahlil at the road's edge.

Rouzbeh paused too. Yet he was not smart enough to end the fight here. He snatched for her pole.

Twisting as her father had taught her, Wu brought up the other end of her staff fast. It struck Rouzbeh across the ear. She followed through with a hardier thwack to his other ear.

He fell to the dust and grit.

Kahlil ran toward Najih's other wards in the olive grove and yelled, "She hit him! The mute hit Rouzbeh!"

His thin pride shattered, Rouzbeh wore his regret briefly. Hatred and determination returned to his features. He clutched the left side of his face, got to his feet, and peeled away.

Wu let him go and watched with her chin held high. She didn't waste her voice on him and his kind. Her actions spoke for her. She delivered the same challenging glare to the orphans watching from the ridge above. They didn't all deserve it. But she could never guess who Rouzbeh or Najih would spoil with their lies, their hate for the Creb.

When the others began heading to Kruispad with their loads over their shoulders, Wu patched the hole in her basket as best she could and gathered what olives were salvageable, enough to keep her from Najih's accusations of laziness. Then she hoisted the baskets once more.

Rouzbeh had disappeared inside the city gate before Wu joined the procession, doubtlessly driven by his eagerness to spin a tale for Najih.

She studied the dunes around the plains by the river as she walked. The daily temptation of salvation called to her, be it death in the maw of a crocodile or welcome from a kind Daijon tribe heading north to civilized Anzante. No. Ekon needed her. She wouldn't risk the desert without her. Ekon had already paid too steep a price.

Thanks to Kahlil's shouts, the others under Najih's thumb gave Wu her space with looks that said, "Invader. Trespasser." Some treated her with respect, former Daijon tribe members themselves. Whatever they thought of her, she carried no shame for her mother's Creb blood and her rosewood-tinted brown skin, nor for the slight bump and length her Creb ancestry had added to her nose.

She gave the desert road a final glance before stepping through the dry wooden gate of Kruispad. As rudely cautious of outsiders as southern Anzanteans were, they never closed their city's gates. A lingering superstition from when the sheikh line had followed the teachings of the old gods. To this day, they believed it brought bad luck to lock out visitors this close to the encroaching desert.

Pedestrians muttered cursed oaths under their breath daily when Najih's wards passed through the packed streets with their long poles across their shoulders. Wu struggled to keep herself close to the end of line, as most of the people didn't notice her following the others, all taller than her by at least a hand. Upon reaching the stench of the butcher's stall and his daily opportunity to spit and grimace at her, Wu knew the end of the journey was near. Turning the corner at the tile-paved road to Najih's white-walled estate, she put her mind off her waning endurance for the weight of the baskets and glanced up to see who guarded the gate that afternoon.

Two guards? Merde.

Feeble Sayed had worn the same dark red chechia with its fraying tassel every day since she and Ekon had first escaped to Kruispad. She had hoped he alone would be on guard that evening. Sayed couldn't hear a mosquito in his ear.

In a white turban with a gold and ruby brooch, this new guard, as robust as his thick mustache, had to be new to the city, almost new to adulthood. Unlike Sayed's yellowing eyes, his harbored a spirited twinkle, even as they roamed keenly over each ward. His desire to prove himself to his overseer didn't dissuade Wu from her plan for the night, though she felt her chance of success dwindling. When she entered his gaze, she set hers on the hilt of his curved short sword, a swift tug away from being free of its gilded sheath. A swift tug away from being hers. Along the sheath, the beautiful curvy, dotted script of Taus relayed a message she couldn't interpret.

Wu abandoned the daydream of taking the sword to Najih's chest as she climbed the short hill up to the estate courtyard. She set her baskets with the others and begrudgingly laid her pole aside as well. Then she skirted around to the back of the group awaiting Najih's inspection of their day's work. This was one instance where her height played to an advantage. She had hidden from Najih's attention for nine days in a row once. Her record.

"Wu," Ekon called quietly. She ran at her from the side door to Najih's residence, leaving the others parted and curious in her wake. Black kohl came to sharp points at the outer edges of her wide eyes. Nothing else was sharp about Ekon, from her perfectly oval head down to her sinuous torso to her clean pink toenails. She had suffered Najih's attention from the start. Forced to marry a man twice as old as her father at age fifteen, Ekon's face had often held a haunted chill since.

Each day Wu gave thanks for her not falling pregnant.

Seizing Wu's arms, Ekon said, "You must run! Get away from here! They will kill you!" She had rounded her accent, like so many things she had changed to gain Najih's favor. Ekon waited for a reaction, but Wu didn't know what to say. It couldn't possibly be a revelation to her. Ekon knew of the scars on her hands. "Wu?" She lowered her voice to a sound barely strong enough to survive the distance. "Do you not even speak to me now?"

"Ekon!" Najih barked. "Get away from that flea."

Ekon's arms fell straight to her side.

Already dressed in his draping white jibba and layered red silk scarves for the great feast, Najih hauled Rouzbeh out of his manor. "Look what she has done!" His fat hand turned Rouzbeh's face to display the purple welt Wu's staff had left.

Wu tried not to grin behind Ekon's back.

As soon as Ekon stepped aside, Wu's eyes fell to the tan courtyard tiles.

"Give me your hands," Najih ordered.

Choking her fear in her throat, Wu flinched away instinctually.

He snatched her hands and squeezed them hard. His thumbs traveled the scars he had left on her skin. "You get another line for this. Where shall I put it, hmm?"

Despite her best effort, she trembled. She focused on the hem of Najih's jibba. Red beads adorned it between rubies. Seven more were bound to the toes of his jeweled slippers.

Najih ducked close and said, "I still owe you one, do I not?"

"Najih," Ekon murmured, "have you approved my new kaftan for the feast, my love?" The polished ruby he had placed on Ekon's marriage finger moved closer to light on his arm. Her lips smiled sweetly for their captor. "I thought I could wear it with my diamond collar? I would love to model it for you before tonight."

His wine-scented breath stopped falling on Wu's face. He shifted and let her go.

Wu swiftly joined her hands behind her back.

"Lock her away," Najih said to Rouzbeh. "I will punish her later."

Shame hid in plain sight on Ekon's face. She didn't meet Wu's eyes as they went inside. Had the man truly known her or truly loved her, he would have seen it. He'd have known he could never touch Ekon's heart.

Rouzbeh grabbed Wu's arm and hauled her along to the orphans' quarters, a long wooden shack built off an old square tower just large enough to hide away Najih's problems.

Unable to help herself, Wu glanced up to the white, yellow, and blue pennant flags running from the tower to the neighbors' home and so on through the district in a show of unity for Anzante.

Pride for Anzante was a strange concept for her. Her tribe had lived in this country her entire life, even paid taxes for land they would never have claimed to own, but Anzante had never offered her anything in return. Its boast of being a free nation of beautiful coasts and hospitality fell short near its borders and ignored the ignorant strife in the south.

Rouzbeh dragged her into the large room she shared with twenty-six of her conscripted peers, where more than one blanket was permitted only when someone vanished and then only until it was discovered. Wu liked to believe those who had disappeared had taken their chances with the desert and the roaming slavers. But she knew in her gut more than one of the children had died at the hand holding her arm now. Most of them had had fairer skin than the average Anzantean, though few had received as many scars as she had.

Up the rickety, dry wooden stairs they climbed to the top of the tower. Rouzbeh flung open the new steel-reinforced door Najih had purchased and dragged her inside the tiny room. He pressed her against the wall and bent down over her. "You won't survive next time. You won't even see me coming."

The longer she held her breath, the more her temptation grew to trip him out of the open window, though she knew Ekon's sacrifice could not save her from Najih's retaliation. As Rouzbeh lingered, she knew where his mind wandered. She'd take him beyond the veil with her before she would let that happen.

He spit on her and let go.

She scowled back at him and wiped her cheek on her shoulder.

Once he stood on the landing, she slammed the door closed for him. Then she stood away from it and braced herself for a fight until she heard the lock slide into place.

"You're dead, flea," he said through the door. "One less filthy invader."

Edging her view forward to spy out of the window, she waited for Rouzbeh to cross the courtyard three stories below. When he returned to the others and began helping pack the olives for the pressers and merchants, she curled up on the bare wooden floor and tucked her arm under her head. It was going to be difficult to sleep knowing what the city had in store for her that evening. Retreating to her daydreams, she grinned.

Drums woke her. Sleep had come to comfort her after all, though the floor had been less kind to her shoulder. Starry darkness had begun to suck the heat of the day away. Knowing Najih would be at the feast near the university before the entertainment had begun, she scanned the empty courtyard below.

Najih had had the rough surface of the tower smoothed down below the window to prevent his prisoners from climbing to their freedom. She smirked and shook her head. Why had he assumed they would climb down?

Reaching out to the left, Wu stepped up on the window's ledge and found her grip. She set the edge of her sandal on another outcropping brick beneath it and pressed it down with her big toe. Then she swung her weight out over the height. With a small leap, she snagged the rope suspending the pennant flags. As she often did to the branches when picking olives, she raised her legs and crossed them over the rope. Her backward descent to the neighbor's house was slow and cautious, more for fear of drawing anyone's eyes than for the height itself. This wasn't her most graceful method of escape from the estate, but it had never failed her before. Despite the festival lasting only three nights, she could take advantage of the decorations all week if needed. None of the neighbors wanted to be the first to break the sign of unity.

She dropped to the neighbor's low roof and skipped along. Then she hopped to their servants' shack and jumped to the property wall. Wu darted atop the walls between the estates toward the market and finally climbed down onto crates in an alleyway. An advantage of being small in the dimly lit streets, hardly anyone noticed her, and fewer would notice the Creb in her features.

For a few seconds, she stared in wonder at the heaping bowls of orange, yellow, and red spices in the corner market stalls. Mounds of ground herbs had been replenished for the week of feasts too. The aroma had her mouth watering.

Under the drums and the chatting patrons of the market, Wu felt invisible. Dodging goats and elbows, she skulked through the warren of narrow pathways on her way to the one face that always greeted her with a smile. Delicious scents wafted from the bakeries as she passed, mostly overcoming the stink of the fearful animals awaiting the butcher's knife.

Avoiding the area of the city restricted to men, she wound her way close to the university, the southernmost known in the "civilized" lands. All local, the young men took turns playing the buzuq on a stage in the university square. Before them, the wealthy, including Najih, sat on large, fine rugs and dined from platters between neighbors. Najih's belly shook with a laugh louder than the music. Ekon barely smiled and stared at the food before her without eating.

To stay out of sight, Wu ducked under the tables of the few stalls set up to sell to the university's students and crawled. Around the corner, she spotted Rafit emptying a bowl of roasted nuts onto a mound to be offered for dessert. The intricately woven beads of his white and green Daijon necklace clacked together as he righted the bowl in his hands. He gave his work a satisfied nod.

When she first had found him, Wu had harbored hope he could get her and Ekon out of Kruispad. But while Rafit was Daijon, he was tribeless and remained in the city year-round.

She shuffled out behind him.

Hearing the rustle, Rafit turned and grinned through his white beard. She loved the way his beard stood out against his dark skin and how his right front tooth crossed over his left. "Bon soir, mon petit chou!" he said in her father's accent. Her accent. Hearing it stirred a wonderful, sad pain. "I have been waiting to share a surprise with you! Come." He pointed his elbow to the back of his stall.

Wu squatted under a table again and took the lead, but she waited for him to arrive and peel back the towel hiding the treasure on a copper plate. Normally, when she could sneak away, Rafit saved her some of his tagine. But the feasts always brought new surprises and sometimes her old favorites from the ports up north.

With a broad grin, Rafit whipped away the towel.

Seasoned lamb, chicken with mashed garbanzo beans, and two different mounds of rice waited for her inhale. One mound of rice smelled of tomatoes and garlic. The green one she couldn't identify.

Rafit plopped a flatbread over the spiced lentils in the center of the plate and put the bounty into her hands. "Remember now, little one," he said, patting his fist over his heart twice, "our secret."

She nodded and patted her heart twice in promise. Feeling the warmth of his smile on her the whole way, Wu scurried away from the feast and down to the river just at the edge of the music. With her copper plate cautiously balanced to avoid dropping a single grain of rice, Wu flipped off her sandals and waded into to the river's cooling pull. She found a perch on a thick old bridge post and lazily kicked the water with her feet. The new bridge carried the busy noise of the city overhead.

This was her sanctuary, the only place in Kruispad where she dared to remember her life before Najih, before the Ghost. With Rafit's cooking, it was easier to imagine her parents sharing her meal with her. Her father had not enjoyed the raisins in the rice last year, but her mother had gladly eaten them all. This year her mother reminded Wu the Creb called garbanzo beans "chickpeas," which made her grin.

Then Wu began her lessons in Common under her mother's tutelage.

She tried to recall as many words as her mother had taught her, especially those closest to the end of their time together. Halfway through her meal, Common interrupted her lesson.

"I found it, Bapu!" a girl shouted.

Wu stopped chewing.

Under the torchlight from the bridge, a dark-haired girl with skin the color of wet sand ran into view at the opposite edge of the shallow river. She cried out again. Dressed in orange pantaloons and a short yellow shirt, the girl excitedly waved back up to the road.

Strange men with long beards under their turbans answered her summons to the water's edge. Spread out in a line, the strangers in pleated and pied clothing invaded Wu's sanctuary and washed their hands and faces with a glee only traveling the desert could conjure.

Wu studied the girl.

Despite her innocent cheer, she couldn't have been much younger than Wu, if at all. A red, a green, and a gold pouch dangled from a golden silk cord belt around the girl's waist. She placed the pouches on her lap and squatted over the water. Her fingers dipped into the river, then rubbed her smiling face. She splashed the man next to her.

Droplets caught in his white beard, combed to part in the center. He released a deep laugh and scooped up a handful of water in retaliation.

"No, Bapu!" she cried in protest.

The fight ended in laughter when he returned a thoroughly drenching wave.

As some of the refreshed travelers brought their merchant wagons to rest under the palms across the water, others began building fires and stringing up brightly colored tents between the carts.

Swallowing her bite of spiced lentils, Wu realized she'd caught the girl's attention.

The stranger's smile grew. She waved excitedly.

Wu stood, brushed off her seat, and walked away to find some privacy. After all, the fool had to learn. You had to work for your welcome in Kruispad.

Chapter 3: Mangoes Make the Summer

The lock on the tower door rattled, waking Wu. She rose into a crouch near the window, prepared to hurl herself at Rouzbeh or one of his loyal fools if they had come with ill intent.

A girl half Wu's age opened the door and ran back down the stairs. Stunned that Rouzbeh hadn't sought his revenge, Wu squatted there in the morning sun and tried to recall the girl's name. No. She'd never known it. It had been months since the girl had joined Najih's fold, claiming her parents had been taken by the Ghost in the dunes, but Wu had no idea what her name was. How distant had she become to ignore one whose story matched her own?

She stretched and let the thought go. There were better occupations for her mind. Though he hadn't acted first thing this morning, Rouzbeh must have prepared a new plan, now that she had given him a real offense to feed his hate.

Downstairs, she passed through the stale air of the long shack and the mostly empty bowls of gruel being collected by the youngest servants. Again, she was thankful for Rafit's generosity. Outside, more of the young ones fed the chickens they were forbidden to touch.

Wu kept her eyes keen for Rouzbeh, Kahlil, or any of the boys swayed by fear or hate to do as Najih would. Collecting a wooden pole from the stack gave her some small comfort. She opted to carry her baskets in her left hand, should she need to use the stave as a weapon, and made her way to the loosely formed, heavy-footed line outside the estate gate. When she finally spotted Rouzbeh, she added weight to her own step and idled on occasion behind the tallest of the olive pickers.

Once in the field, she sought shelter high in the boughs of the centuries-old trees at the heart of the grove, where a few children would spend their entire day collecting olives from the generous aged branches. As she worked, expertly tossing her pickings into her baskets, Wu balanced her pole in her lap.

Only once during the day did Rouzbeh draw near enough to send her climbing barefoot up to the highest branches with the thickest silvery-green foliage. He didn't see her and moved on.

Regardless, she kept a sharp eye and minded her surroundings, seldom dallying in daydreams of what the night might bring as her fingers worked. Rafit gladly spoiled her when the city's trade was good, which it should remain for another week still.

Finally ready to surrender the tree's shelter, Wu spied through the branches to the date palms barely peeking over the hill to the south under the pinking sky. The darkest of her nightmares lay beyond that distant grove, still abducting tribes and selling them off as slaves. Why would no one stop the Ghost? But then, who could?

After a glance to check the height of the olives in her baskets, Wu surveyed the orchard. Rouzbeh was nowhere to be seen. She dropped down, slipped her sandals on, and gathered her baskets before sprinting to the road, closely trailing those she knew would not succumb to Rouzbeh's intimidation.

Outside the estate gate, the new guard spotted her and drew up. He looked to the sky. His hand rose for her to stop. "You are early, little one. You wish to rile him?" Then he looked beyond her.

The others, including Rouzbeh and Kahlil, approached in the winding alley.

The guard swung the gate open for them. His black eyes tried to deliver an undecipherable message to Wu as she passed.

Uphill, Najih had company in the courtyard.

Wu froze upon recognizing the priest of Mulgrum, Priest Josiah, the same priest who had handed her and Ekon over to Najih. Wu, like most of those belonging to the estate, had thought seeking shelter from the god of the oasis to be their best choice. Now she knew just how deadly wrong she had been.

When she had escaped with Ekon during their first night at Najih's estate and had run crying to the priest, he had turned them back over immediately. That was the night Najih had given her the first scar, straight over her right knuckles. He wanted it to hurt, for her to remember her place and what happened when she stepped outside it.

Someone nudged her from behind.

Wu settled her baskets in the row for sorting and kept watch out of the corner of her eye. The fat priest had brought another ward for Najih. The tan boy couldn't be older than ten. More Creb than hers, his long nose stood out from his face in a defined point.

The boy pulled against Najih's merciless hold on his arm. A fast slap ended his defiance but not his weeping.

Priest Josiah disregarded the punishment and turned to go.

She averted her eyes to avoid his. No piety awaited her there, only the promise of another night in the tower for disrespecting Najih's guest. And she much preferred the loose board sealing the hole in the wall behind the coop to scaling over the neighbor's house.

Raw flesh surrounded the boy's wrists. He sniveled uncontrollably. That would only serve to put Najih further under his demons. At this rate, the boy would take the tower room for the night, if Rouzbeh didn't get to him first. A harsh fate to what he, too, must have hoped was an end to his nightmare.

"Silence yourself now," Najih threatened, "or I shall make you weep for days."

Wu steeled herself with a deep breath. To the others' astonishment, and her own inward cringe, she heeled a basket hard, sending it rolling down the entry and spilling olives by the dozens as far as the gate.

Najih didn't bother with a warning. He spread his shadow over her, seized her arm, and drew his hand up to backhand her but stopped.

The priest and the guard watched from the gate. While the priest promptly ignored the scene and carried on, Najih's new guard watched with uncertainty.

Najih shoved her toward the tower. When she stumbled, he dragged her.

Wu searched the onlookers for Ekon but found her trepidation mirrored amid the lowered glances. The dread is worse than the pain. The dread is worse than the pain.

Out of the hot sun, Najih hauled her inside the shack and up to the tower room. He slung her to the wooden planks before him and drew his knife.

Wu whimpered despite herself and scooted back to the window ledge.

"That's what I like to hear," Najih said. "Now tell me you're sorry."

She found her resolve in her anger and stood up straight. Her every muscle fought not to shiver for the man's enjoyment.

"No?" He studied the back of her right hand. "I think here is where we left off." Without hesitation, his blade arced over the back of her hand, leaving a deep cut, deeper than normal. She couldn't stop her abrupt inhale or her tears, but her mouth clamped closed.

He shoved her into the wall and, when she fell, spat on her. "Filthy, trespasser."

Wu lay there, hiding her tears, until she heard the lock. Working in a spiral, she tore a long strip from her right pant leg. Hardly suited for rags, the material tore easily. Gently but tightly, she bound the wound. Pretending it hadn't been cut so deeply, she held her hand to her chest and scooted closer to the window to feel the breeze on her wet face.

Down in the courtyard, the new arrival now hid, absorbed deeply in the others waiting for dismissal. They always tried at first. Then, when it came down to standing up to Rouzbeh or Najih, they sacrificed the lamb. But not with Wu. She was never a lamb.

Najih barked something that sent them running to their chores.

Wu lay back on the sun-warmed floor and tried to clear her mind to rest.

Sleep did not find her amid her shivers.

A boom startled her upright with her arms wrapped about her. Green sparkles blinked out in the starry sky through the window. The second feast had begun, this one honoring Mulgrum.

Why had the wind gone so cold?

Briefly, she considered forgoing tonight's freedom. But her stomach overcame her caution. Her hand mostly hurt when she closed it. She could use her elbow on the rope, if needed.

Wu leaned out to spy the guard's position. With him nowhere in sight, she stepped up to the ledge. Her hand throbbed with the use of her fingers, but she managed her climb through the biting wind to the rope.

With her legs wrapped around the pennant line, weakness washed through her. She crooked her elbow around the rope and relaxed her wounded hand.

A sensation of being watched stirred the fine hairs on her neck. The guard stood at the gate. Wu shallowed her breathing. Whether he watched her, she couldn't say. But he stared up through the gate at something. Her muscles began to ache. She closed her eyes to summon her strength. When she opened them, he was gone.

She hurriedly finished her descent. After dropping into the alleyway, she wiped her sweaty face on her short sleeve. The gaiety of Mulgrum's festival echoed around the corners. It didn't lift her spirits as high as it had the night before. Still, she ran through the crowded streets, the fragrant spice stalls, and the mouth-watering aroma of roasted lamb to the music-filled university square.

Rafit's face split into a wide smile for her. It diminished when he noticed the bloody bandage around her hand, though he pretended not to. He waved her around to the back. "Come, come." He lifted the lid of an earthenware pot to reveal her favorite: chicken and dried apricot tagine studded with garbanzo beans. Raisins had been mounded on one of side of the dish as a treat.

With a grateful smile, she patted her chest and accepted her copper plate.

As she turned to go, Rafit said, "One more thing." He placed a small brown wafer on the raisins. "Dessert." A second disk appeared in his hand, which he gave to her.

She frowned at the chocolate. It wasn't new to her, having been her mother's favorite.

"Go on. Try it. I promise you will love it!"

Wu bit off a small piece of the creamy sweetness and chewed. She grinned as convincingly as she could and set the remainder of the wafer with the other on her plate.

With his own victorious grin, Rafit said, "I knew you would love it! Now, eat before it gets cold, you hear me?" His eyes lit on her hand again, but she left without explanation. Their friendship had always been a simple one. Why muddy it now?

After a pensive walk to her sanctuary under the bridge, Wu paused to make sure she was truly alone before kicking off her sandals. She quietly made her way through the cold water to her perch. A little too cold, Wu picked her feet up out of the water and rested them on the post in front of her.

The merchant caravan across the shallow river bustled with men from the university exploring wares from beyond the desert. The pupils who had come to study in Kruispad were always more curious than the locals. Amid the bright lantern light casting shapes of stars and moons on their tents, the men in turbans casually urged their customers into a sale. Every time they were successful, they released a hardy laugh and patted the buyer hard on the back. One young man bought a large curved sword and nearly toppled over from the mirthful slap. Another who had purchased a glass vial of an unidentifiable brown juice received a wink and subtle nod instead.

Halfway through her meal, Wu stared at her plate. She couldn't put her finger on it, but something was off about the tagine. Rafit often had a heavy hand when adding spices and garlic, yet this dish had little flavor.

Perhaps she was coming down with something. She did feel weak and had been daydreaming about curling up in the sun rather than running through her mother's lessons in Common.

"Ohyee!" a cheerful voice said behind her.

Wu started and jerked her head around.

The girl from the caravan had trapped her. She waded out in her orange pantaloons to where Wu sat and, when Wu moved her feet, hopped up to sit on the post across from her, blocking Wu's view of the bartering with her smiling face. "May I join you? My name is Madhu." When Wu didn't reply, the girl asked, "Oh, are you mute?"

Nodding, Wu looked away from the brightness in Madhu's eyes.

"You don't have to talk," Madhu said, though Wu could hear disappointment in her voice. She brought her damp legs up to her chest and wrapped her arms around them. "I listen to people all day. It'd be nice to be heard instead." Her face slackened when she spotted Wu's bandaged hand. She pointed at it. "Did you hurt yourself?"

Wu hid her injured hand under her plate and gave a simple nod.

"That's a lot of blood," the girl said. "Would you like a clean bandage? I can get one."

As Wu considered the offer, her eyes drifted closed. Too long. When she opened them, the girl stood before her.

Madhu lifted Wu's plate and set it on the post where she had been sitting. Then she put the back of her hand to Wu's forehead. She sucked a fast breath through her teeth. "You have a fever! Ahyee . . ." She glanced down at Wu's bandaged hand and reached for it. Wu snapped it away. "Your cut is probably infected."

After searching the shore behind them, Madhu said, "Wait here, all right? Do not leave!" She ran through the shallow water to her caravan.

A fever? Her shivering made sense now. Wu entertained the idea of making an escape but opted to stay. Fever and infection killed most around here. If Madhu had medicine, she'd need it to survive. A bandage not torn from her soiled linens would be nice too.

Several minutes passed before Madhu reappeared carrying a bronze tray by its wooden handles. She waded in and set it atop one of the posts. "You drink this while I mix the ingredients." She handed Wu a delicate cup with a pale, warm tea of some kind.

Sniffing the concoction, Wu didn't recognize it.

"Yarrow tea," Madhu explained. "It's good for the fever. Drink, drink."

Bitter yet slightly sweet, the tea was not as pleasant as Wu had thought it might be, what with the way the few Racinians she had seen in her time had refused to go a day without it. But then, there were few things about Racinians that made sense to kind hearts.

Watching out of the corner of her eye, Madhu winced. "Does it need more honey?" She reached for a small ceramic container until Wu shook her head.

Sliding a mortar to the center of the tray, Madhu began working. She tore apart a leafy herb and dropped it inside. As she pestled, she said, "We are in luck. The witch hazel has survived our travels better than I would have thought." Her fingers pinched a pouched substance and sprinkled a bit into the mix.

Unwrapping her hand, Wu groaned slightly. The sticky fabric pulled at the cut. Slowly and steadily, she eased it free. She let the bloodied strip fall and ride the current north. Dipping her hand into the water, Wu let it rinse the wound.

Madhu tipped the mortar, displaying a dark lump of mush. "This is a medicine my nanni makes."

The scent of the witch hazel conjured memories of the time her mother had used it on Gbad'Herdu when he'd been injured on the hunt. Wu had forgotten about that until now.

Madhu removed the lid from the honey and poured more than Wu could afford to repay. "Feverfew, witch hazel, myrrh gum, and honey. I will not tell Bapu about the myrrh, if you do not." She grinned.

Wide-eyed, Wu felt herself pale. How much would this cost? Could she ever repay it?

To make matters worse, Madhu spread out a fine brown linen cloth and mounded the medicine onto it. Gingerly taking Wu's arm, she said, "I'm sorry; this may sting."

Wu braced herself, but it didn't hurt at all. It felt slimy and dirty, but she trusted the remedy she knew her mother had used.

Having tied off the bulky bandage, Madhu brought up Wu's other hand and rubbed her thumb over the scars. Her eyes spoke volumes, but she simply said, "Both hands." She released her. "Come, we must see to your fever directly."

Wu's questioning glance went unobserved as Madhu guided her back to the shore.

"Sit," Madhu said, pointing to the water. "Yes, I am serious." She brought Wu's wrapped hand up. "Keep this dry and sit. I will help you."

Wu shook her head. It was far too cold! She backed away.

"It's not cold. It only feels that way because of your fever. It plays tricks on you. Keep your hand dry." Madhu guided her down into the water and sat with her in the current. She grabbed Wu's shoulder when Wu tried to stand again and held her low. "Ahyee. We have to keep your temperature down. Sit!"

Wu's teeth began to chatter.

"It's hard to believe this is the end of summer," Madhu said. "It's too dry, and there are no mangoes, except the ones we brought with us." Madhu fished around in her pocket under the water. Her hand brought out an oblong yellow-and-green fruit that appeared sunburned red on the top. Her other hand freed the small copper knife at her belt. "Do you like mangoes?"

Wu shrugged. She'd never seen one before.

"You can have some, when you are feeling well enough to eat."

"Madhu!" a deep voice bellowed.

"I am here, Bapu!"

The large, white-bearded man Madhu had splashed the night before came to her call and peered into the darkness under the bridge. "Ah, you have found a friend. Good. But why are you sitting in the water?"

"We are staying cool," Madhu said.

"Very well, Daughter. Stay close and hang your clothes up to dry when you finish. It will not do to have them mildew." As he wandered away, he said, "If that is something to fear in this part of the world, I do not know."

Cutting and eating her sweet-smelling mango, Madhu stayed silent for a while after he left.

The fruit smelled divine, but Wu focused her energy on clenching her teeth together and staying warm.

Finished, Madhu held the thick center of the fruit in her hand. "Do you think this would grow here?"

Wu had been wondering the same thing. Despite being forced into labor, she did enjoy seeding the dates and picking the olives. Her tribe had traveled too often to ever take up farming crops that required such attention.

"Let us find out," Madhu said. She stuck her knife into the end and wedged it apart. Gently, she removed the seed from inside. After leaving Wu with a warning stare for her to remain seated in the water, Madhu dug near the river away from the bridge. When she finished, she dropped the seed in and covered it. Running back to the water, she dropped in. "It is a funny thought. I may never know if it grows, but someone someday may find this strange tree with weird fruit and wonder where it came from. A gift from the gods maybe?" She giggled and turned her attention to meticulously cleaning her knife.

They sat in silence again for some time, eavesdropping on students passing overhead, excitedly sharing the mint chutney bread they'd purchased from the caravan.

Flicking the surface of the water, Madhu asked, "How old are you? Seventeen years?"

Wu shook her long curls.

"I am," Madhu said. She grinned. "No, I am not. At the end of the summer, I will be. Sixteen?"

Wu nodded.

"I thought so. Same age, we were fated to be friends. Can you read and write?"

Again, Wu nodded. Her mother's child had no other option.

"Ohyee, you can tell me your name later. I was worried I'd have to guess. I am terrible at that task in foreign countries. Half of the things I say I'm afraid are offensive."

Unable to stop her grin, Wu sniffed a laugh. She had to admit the life of a traveling merchant's daughter appealed to her. Her own tribe traveled through Anzante with the seasons, but, as different as they were, Port Nord on the Saratial Sea and Khadra in the deserts to the south were not exactly exotic. That is, they were not the snow-covered mountains and lake-filled dales of her mother's stories about her homelands. Nor were they the jungles of the hunting legends her father collected.

Clearing the wonder from her mind, Wu felt her face fall forlorn. That life appealed to her. But to attain it, she'd have to traverse the desert and pay the price she swore she never would: abandon Ekon.

She twisted, dug the forefinger of her free hand into the loamy soil behind her, drew her name, and pointed at herself.

"Wu?" Madhu asked. "I never would have guessed that. So, how are you feeling, Wu? Better?"

She was, now that Madhu had called her attention to it.

"You should finish eating," she said, standing. "The spice will help your body sweat out the sickness." She helped Wu back to her post and passed over her copper plate.

The tagine was cold but delicious, its usual flavors graciously restored.

From the depths of her thoughts, Madhu said, "In our home, every year, we celebrate the rain this week." She leaned over to glance up from under the bridge to the starry sky and held out her hand. Then she sighed and shrugged with a grin. "At least we'll have our feast tomorrow. Come eat with us! Be my guest!"

Her pulse quickening with excitement, Wu glanced down to her bandaged hand. Could she? Not if she was forced to take another's place in the tower. She couldn't trust her hand now, especially if infection had rooted in the wound. Realizing she might even be too weak to fight off Rouzbeh tomorrow, she shook her head and tried to relay her genuine regret in her expression, though it felt inadequate.

Madhu nodded to Wu's plate. "I know they're going to make tagine. Bapu wanted to try it." She put her hand to the side of her mouth. "Without the apricots. He doesn't like them. Or dates. I don't know what's wrong with the man."

Smiling, Wu still declined.

Madhu slumped. "It is fine. I understand. I know your people are wary of foreigners."

Wu vehemently shook her head. She wanted to explain. Her mouth opened but closed. Part vow to only speak to those worthy of hearing her and part survival to draw less attention with her Daijon accent, she had hidden her voice deep within for so long now . . . "S'il vous plaît." Her voice was weak. Broken. It was obvious Madhu tried to contain her surprise. "I cannot because I am not permitted."

"I permit you," Madhu said lightly.

Wu didn't know what to say, where to begin her explanation. Spotting the whole chocolate wafer on her plate, she picked it up and offered it to Madhu. "I promise to try. Mais . . . If I fail, please accept this as my apology and my thanks. Merci."

"Ohyee!" Madhu said excitedly. "That's so nice! You don't have to, Wu."

Wu insisted. She didn't want it regardless.

"Nanni will be so thrilled to know her medicine can cure the mute." Madhu teased her with a knowing smile. She raced through the water toward her caravan, then spun. "You will try, you promised."

"I will do everything I can to escape tomorrow aussi—also." Grinning, Wu finished her meal and hoped she'd have the strength to climb back up to the tower when she was done.

Chapter 4: The Tabari Travelers

Wu woke in the morning sun, refreshed and still full from the tagine. Her ascension to the tower window had given her trouble, but she had managed it with only a few scares. Perhaps she would be able to join Madhu tonight after all and explore the foreign wares for herself.

An exciting thought came to her. She dismissed it. Still, it resurfaced to bring a smile to her face. Would Madhu's people be willing to take her and Ekon away?

Two bangs on the door startled her. Wu stood away from it as the lock rattled open.

Rouzbeh flung it open and sneered. "Time to work, trespasser." Holding the door open, he forced her to pass by him.

Wu hurried down the stairs in case he decided to shove her. She kept her pace up through the shack.

Outside, their emptied baskets and poles had been stacked by the gate as usual. With her pole in hand, she upturned her baskets. Two small hands wrapped around her from behind. She jerked upright.

The Creb-Daijon boy smiled up at her. "I know what you did for me," he said. "The others told me you saved me from punishment. Merci. I am Arun."

Wu shoved the boy back. If Rouzbeh saw, it would only serve to make him a target that much faster. She searched for Rouzbeh. Thankfully, the fat-lipped fool hadn't noticed. He was too busy plotting something with Kahlil.

Surprise and hurt filled Arun's eyes. He feared her now. She reached for his shoulders, but he dodged and hid behind the others.

Wu hoped this was not the way her day would continue to play out. However, Rouzbeh's close follow along the road to the southern gate suggested a dark day had just begun.

Just before the city guard at the gate, Wu knelt. She pretended to correct and retie her sandal straps until Rouzbeh passed her by. Even he wouldn't create a scene there. If he did, the guards would bring them both back before Najih for punishment, and Najih was seldom gentler to his motherless bastards.

Keeping a fair distance, Wu now trailed Rouzbeh with little concern for anything else.

"Ohyee!"

Wu tensed and searched behind her.

"There you are," Madhu said, skipping to Wu's side from inside the city gate. "Are you feeling better?"

"Oui," Wu said quietly. "Merci, Madhu. I will see you later, remember?" She walked on.

Missing Wu's point, Madhu said, "I'll walk with you."

Wu halted and kept an eye on Rouzbeh, who had yet to notice them. "No, Madhu. I must work."

"Picking olives?"

"Oui. I will see you this evening." She gave a small smile and displayed her still-bandaged hand. "Thank you again for last night. It feels much better this morning. But I must go."

"I understand," Madhu said with a frown. "But what happens if it rains?" To Wu's amused scoff, she replied, "It is summer. These things happen."

"It does not rain here in summer. Not often. Go back to Kruispad before you get us into trouble."

"Into trouble?"

Wu pleaded with a dire expression and carried on.

Madhu fell behind. She whispered something. When Wu paused to look back, Madhu's back was to her, her attention on something in her hands.

"What are you doing?"

Madhu spun around with a guilty grin on her face. "Nothing." A faint white cloud wafted from the hand behind her back.

"What was that?"

Her strange new friend shook her head and hurried to her side. "But what do you do when it rains?"

"Chores. The olives are sorted. Some used for oil. Some for perfume. The list goes on."

Groaning, Madhu kicked a stone off the path. "I think today you should leave that to the others. You have a friend in town for only a few days."

"How could I leave it?" Wu asked. "Najih would notice I was missing. Rouzbeh would tell him, of this I am certain."

Curtly, Madhu made a face at her. "Did they do that to your hand?"

Wu inhaled deeply and noticed Rouzbeh had already moved out of sight into the grove. "Oui."

Rolling thunder drowned out her answer. Heavy rain pattered the ground ahead of them as it chased the olive pickers back toward the city.

A playful grin crossed Madhu's face. She grabbed Wu's arm and pulled her along until they both sprinted through the gate. "That is strange," Madhu yelled through the downpour. "I heard it doesn't rain here in summer."

Madhu ducked under a shepherd's wagon. Wu swung her baskets under and did the same.

The others never looked their way as they ran by back to the estate.

Wu watched Rouzbeh go. "How did you do this, Madhu? Are you a magus?"

Glancing around, Madhu leaned in to whisper, "You mustn't tell anyone. I'm not supposed to do magic away from my bapu." She wore a withering look. "Westerners get very strange about magic."

"You changed the weather?"

Flinging the comment away, Madhu said, "It's a small thing. It'll fade by early afternoon." She held her palm out to catch some of the deluge and frowned. "It's heavy, but it doesn't reach very far. Not very useful except for watering crops."

"I've never heard of magic like that."

Madhu shrugged and tucked her wet brown hair behind her ear, revealing three golden hoops in her lobe. "We have better archives than these 'civilized' countries. Merith never ruled our kind, so they never burned them."

"Never? I thought Merith ruled everywhere."

"No. Not us."

"Where are you from exactly?"

Laughing, Madhu raced out into the rain again. "Come on, Wu!"

Taking up her baskets, Wu hurried after her. "Wait, Madhu! I must go back!"

The morning bustle had stilled and confined itself under the long overhangs above the bakeries and market stalls. A few brave souls darted from cover to cover. Wu followed Madhu's giggling dash down the center of the street. The cheerful magus didn't slow until they reached the university square and the edge of her rain cloud. On the dry side, they stopped.

Straight as a wall, the rain split the square. Wu felt a pang of guilt upon seeing Rafit's drenched stall on the vacant side. Onlookers stared in awe at the strange sight, forming a line at the water wall when it didn't budge with the wind. A young man, likely a student, put his hand out into the downpour. The large rain drops pelted the tiles hard enough to splash his sandaled feet.

The magical storm hadn't caught the attention of the students alone. Milling near the edge, a portly old woman with skin a shade browner than charcoal wore the hood of her silver mantle down. She stared up to the sky with a broad smile. Her gray hair had been pulled tight to her scalp and gathered in a small ball at her nape.

An uneasiness stirred in Wu. Something was . . . wrong about that woman. Something untrustworthy, though she couldn't put her finger on it.

Combing her fingers through her damp hair, Madhu said, "I will help you pick olives this afternoon. You can pretend the storm did not deter you. Until then, we can do as we please, yes?"

Succumbing to the risk, Wu cautiously replied, "Oui, but only if you promise to help. Najih will expect a full day's worth." Realizing they had gained the strange old woman's attention, Wu pressed Madhu on toward the bridge to the university gate and her caravan. "I have no coin, but show me your wares, traveler."

"Eh, all right," Madhu agreed. "Then the library?"

Wu cast her a sorrowful glance. "They do not allow my kind in the library here."

"Your kind?"

Lowering her voice, Wu answered, "Half-Creb."

"I don't know what that is."

"Good." Wu gestured her on.

The guards at the gate watched the caravan of foreigners with oddly cheerful expressions. Did Madhu's people fail to charm anyone?

As common as their brightly colored pied clothing, smiles from the traveling traders welcomed a new batch of customers that morning. The few women in the caravan dressed more modestly than Madhu. Sheer veils covered their hair, and silks shrouded their bodies in draping greens and reds. Small gold hoops pierced nearly as many noses as ears. Brown and red tattoos spread lacy patterns over their hands, welcoming the newcomers to browse and directing attention to the finer wares on their laden rugs and tables.

Drawn to the brass platters etched with elephants and songbirds, Wu noticed several porcelain cups painted red and blue or orange and pink to match the male merchant's pied clothing and turbans. A souvenir for interacting with the travelers themselves?

"Daughter," Madhu's father called in his deep voice. Jeweled with a large citrine brooch over his forehead, his orange turban had been cut from the same cloth as Madhu's pantaloons. Her yellow shirt, the same as his billowing silk trousers. "Late to bed and up early enough to finish your chores already?"

Madhu smiled up at him. "I had a friend to meet."

His brown eyes lingered on Wu's bandaged hand. Then he looked her over with sympathy, concern. "Ah, yes. I see. And what is your name, little one?" he asked kindly.

"Wu," Madhu answered.

"Well met, Wu. Raza Rao." He put his palms together and bowed. "You may call me Raza. I pray you enjoy your exploration of our camp. We Tabari are here to sell, but if we make a friend, we consider that a greater success."

As he straightened his back, his eyes verged on admonishment for Madhu. "Later, Daughter, you can explain this strange weather the town is having." His eyebrows rose with warning. "I do not need your mother's strength to know the source of that storm."

Madhu lowered her head. "Ahyee . . ."

His hand went to his back then brought forward a small pair of shears. "You may start your reparations with Babhru. You missed an entire leg yesterday."

"I didn't miss it," Madhu admitted. "I had hoped you wouldn't notice."

"Ah," Raza groaned. His finger prodded giggles out of his daughter. With a smile for her, he said, "For once, do as your father tells you."

Studying her joined fingers, Wu fought down the memory of parting with her father.

Madhu broke her out of her melancholy daze by hauling her away between the tents.

Raza nearly shook the ground with his laugh at the face his daughter threw his way. "If it pleases you, Wu, please stay for a meal."

Wu nodded back appreciatively.

Behind the small tent village the Tabari had made, their horses and camels lounged. Madhu dragged her to a penned group of russet-pelted deer unlike any Wu had seen. Stronger than the horses and taller than the camels, the animals twitched their bright red tails and ears at her approach. Fiery orange whorls decorated the length of their long bodies in patterns so beautiful they would make zebras jealous. Beautiful white-ivory antlers branched out on the heads of several. Less impressed by her, they went about eating their oats.

"Ils sont magnifique!" Wu said. "What are they?"

Disinterested, Madhu went to the tallest and began using the shears her father had given her to snip away small tufts of hair. "Spring backs. They're less magnificent when you have to trim their coats for the heat. Every. Other. Day. Bapu is very particular about Babhru. He has been in our family since my grandfather was an infant. But if he does not hold still, he will never meet mine." Little Madhu glared up at the beast's red iris.

Wu cautiously raised her fingers to touch Babhru's leg. His hair was warm and softer than expected.

"It's tradition," Madhu said. She quit shearing and bent to collect the shorn tufts from the ground. "My people always bring spring backs when we travel."

"Why?"

Madhu threw her a curious expression, then she nodded for Wu to follow her into a white-and-green tent. Burlap sacks sat open in rows, some filled with nuts, others with grain. Madhu went to one half-filled with the russet trimmings from the spring backs. She dropped in her handfuls and brushed off her fingers. "Put your hand in there."

"Pourquoi?"

"Do it. Go on."

Wu sank her hand into the supple red wool. "It is warm! Almost hot."

"It stays warm for years," Madhu said. "We sell it if we must, not that the desert leaves many wanting for coats."

"You may be surprised," Wu said. "I have suffered many cold nights in Kruispad."

Frowning, Madhu nodded. "There is more we gain from the spring backs." She led Wu out and into a sapphire-blue tent. Three women whispered to each other while they sat around a bowl of dates, chopping and laughing. Madhu quietly snuck to the table behind them and pinched off a hunk of what appeared to be a crustless loaf of bread, but the consistency was dense.

Outside the tent, Madhu split the white substance and put half in Wu's hand before eating hers.

Wu studied the gift. "Goat cheese?"

"Eat it," Madhu said, encouraging her with a nod.

Wu did. While it shared its texture with goat cheese, the flavor was entirely new. A sweet heat roamed over Wu's tongue and remained after she had swallowed.

"It is a strange milk to drink," Madhu said, crinkling her nose. "But I like the cheese." It took a moment for Wu to realize it was her smile Madhu returned. "There is much more of this world for you to see, Wu." She splayed her hands in either direction of the makeshift stalls. "What do you want to see next?"

A small chime rang out three times.

"What was that?" Wu asked.

"The first midday meal," Madhu answered. "We take turns eating and minding the wares. Oh, are you hungry? We could eat now."

Loathe to admit it, she was. The spring back cheese had only whetted her appetite. She nodded.

They went back through the blue tent to one adjoining it. Bordered by four other tents, the dining tent had gaps in the roof allowing a gentle breeze from the blue sky. A few men and one woman sat on the cushions arranged around a large bowl with layers of spiced chicken, roasted vegetables, and carrot shavings resting on a bed of yellow saffron rice.

Wu's mouth watered.

Raza swept in behind them with someone in tow. "Welcome! We are fortunate to have so many visitors today." His large hand gently pressed Wu between her shoulder blades. "Sit. Sit. We have plenty."

As she crossed her legs to sit next to Madhu, Wu realized Raza had escorted in the strange old woman from the university square.

After removing her silver mantle, the woman accepted Raza's help down to the cushions. "My, this is quite lovely, isn't it?" she asked Wu in an unmistakably Racinian accent.

Wu jumped to her feet so quickly it startled everyone. She recognized how rude her behavior must appear, but she hurried outside. Crossing the bridge to the university square, she heard Madhu calling out to her.

Rain still poured over most of the city. Wu opted for her sanctuary instead, heading down the slope to the shore and back under the bridge. If Madhu wanted to talk, she could find her there, not tearing bread with a

Racinian. She took her usual perch on the old bridge post and waited, hoping Madhu would follow.

Solace returned to her slowly. While the daylight made her feel exposed, she was pleased she didn't have to fear crocodiles hiding in the shadows.

Sure enough, footsteps sounded in the sandy soil behind her. "So this is where you have been hiding?" a man's voice asked.

Wu shot to her feet, landing with a splash in the shallow river.

Najih's new guard stood on the shore.

Chapter 5: Gbad'Wu

Wu's pulse thundered. Her eyes went to the curved short sword at the guard's waist. She shifted her stance on the loamy soil of the riverbed, ready to flee. But then what? Face the desert alone? Brave the roads north alone? She couldn't abandon Ekon to Najih. She wouldn't. Bracing herself to fight, she set her shoulder for a run at the guard.

The man raised his large hands in peace. "You have nothing to fear from me, little one. I was worried when you did not return with the others. They say Kruispad is where your kind disappear . . ." His expression said he wished he hadn't said that. "Our kind."

Wu blinked at him. There was nothing Creb about him.

"I know I do not look it," he said. "But my grandmother . . ." He nodded and lowered his voice. "She was Creb. My grandfather, a Daijon. If I had stayed with the tribe, I would be Haril'Antomé." He held out an orange tangerine for her to take.

Wu refused to get closer, unsure if she believed him and unwilling to speak her questions.

With a smile, he splayed his hands again. His thick fingers set the plump fruit on an old bridge post. "I thought you must be hungry. 'What if she did not find food when she snuck out of the tower?' I asked myself." His teeth shone in another smile. "Well . . ." He backed away. "The others are too busy to have noticed you are missing. If you want help sneaking in, come to me."

Madhu sidled down the slope of the riverbank behind him with the front of her shirt bowled around fruit and a few flatbreads. For the first time Wu had heard, Madhu's voice went hard. "Who are you?" she asked. Her right hand went to the red pouch dangling from her waist.

Antomé glanced back at her but said to Wu, "A friend."

Madhu skirted around him and stared up into his dark eyes, her fingers working the mouth of her pouch open. Wu thought it strange to see anger on Madhu's clever face. "She's leaving with us," Madhu said sternly and raised the pouch. "I warn you not to test me. I know the fear your kind hold for magic. It is not a fear known to me and the Tabari."

Antomé gave her a friendly smile. "This is good," he said to Wu and pointed at Madhu. "Find your way out of Kruispad. I believe the deserts would be safer for you than Najih Gorondo's groves." With a nod to each of them, he said, "I have said my piece. I will leave you to enjoy your meal."

Never changing her wary expression, Wu watched Antomé ascend the shore.

Madhu followed him a ways up the bank and watched him leave. Then she returned to Wu. "Who was that? Are you all right?"

Wu nodded, suddenly plagued with guilt for her rude departure. "You brought me food after how I treated your guest?"

"I thought I might bribe an explanation out of you," Madhu answered with a grin. She retrieved the tangerine Antomé had left, looked it over, and added it to her bundle.

"She was Racinian," Wu replied with disdain. "Racinians took my mother's peoples' lands. They drove the Creb across the sea and into Anzante one battle at a time until there were only hundreds left."

"Oh. I thought she was nice."

Wu frowned.

"She didn't mention the Creb. Or Racine."

Resuming her usual perch, Wu gestured for Madhu to assume hers across from her. She selected Antome's gifted tangerine from Madhu's bundle and tore it open. A chunk of the peel fell and whirled about her ankle until the current swept it away. "I could not leave with you, Madhu. Ekon needs me here."

"Who?"

"Ekon. She is the last member of my tribe. Besides me." Wu struggled to explain. In her mind, her words shamed her for inaction, her failure to uphold her responsibilites, her father's expectations, her father's legacy as true leader. "I would be the leader of the Gbad tribe." Turning her palms up, Wu said, "My full name is Wu of the Gbad tribe. Gbad'Wu. But my father's tribe did not survive." She pulled her shaking hands back to her lap and straighted up to look Madhu in the eye. "You know of the wandering tribes of Anzante and Taus? The Daijon?"

With a smile, Madhu said, "I like their necklaces. The beads are so pretty."

A small, bittersweet grin crossed Wu's lips at the memory of her mother's hibiscus-colored necklace, the love her father had taken to lay the message across its strands so delicately. "Oui. They are my people."

She ate a wedge from the tart tangerine and another as she gathered her thoughts. "It was unusual for our tribe to come this far south. Mais . . . Gbad'Turu had fallen ill. Her sickness grew worse day after day. In Pulasa, a man came to my father with rumors that promised a cure could be found in a plant flourishing in the satyr ruins just inside the desert." She looked upstream to the south. Shame heated her cheeks at the thought they should have let Gbad'Turu die. "It was a trap."

Hiding her shaking lips, she devoured the rest of the tangerine while

Madhu waited patiently with eyes too caring to look at. Wu swallowed. "There were no plants there in the desert. We should have known. Stupid. Foolish. Innocent. Slavers, that is what we found."

Madhu reached forward and put her hand on Wu's arm.

Wu flinched, frightening Madhu's touch away. "Je suis désolé, Madhu." She grinned reassuringly and took some of the flatbread to occupy her fidgeting hands. "My tribe did not survive." Her hand lowered the torn bread away from her lips. "My father sacrificed himself so that Ekon and I could escape."

Weakened at the notion of leaving Ekon in Kruispad, Wu hunched over and rested her elbows on her knees. "Even if the Gbad tribe is no more, I will not leave Ekon. She saved my life that night. She has saved me many times since."

This time, Wu did not flinch when Madhu rubbed her shoulder. "What do you mean?" Madhu asked. "If you and Ekon survived, your tribe still exists."

Shaking her head, Wu sat up. "The symbol of the Daijon tribes is the weapon of their leader. My father's spear is in the hands of the Ghost." If he still has it.

"Ghost?"

"The leader of the slavers. A dangerous magus. He paints his face white and wears bones as jewelry that he rattles." It felt good to share the horror, even if it did no good in solving their predicament.

"That is why it is my responsibility to see Ekon freed from Najih." Finally, she allowed herself to admit, "But I do not know how. Every attempt has only led to scars." She flung up her bandaged hand.

"I do. I know how." Madhu stood in the current with her shirt still bundling what food remained. "First, we get your father's spear back. Maybe we can find your parents and set them free?"

"No," Wu replied. "It has been years, Madhu. I saw my father die. My mother . . . gone. Sold or dead. Or sold and dead." Her lips tightened to squeeze the mourning shivers from them.

"Years?" Madhu leaned back against her post. "You have been living with that Najih for so long?"

Nodding, Wu said, "Oui. We thought when we found Kruispad, the people would come to our aid. But they ignored us. I thought . . . je ne sais pas . . . I thought the priests of the old gods would show compassion and gather others to save our tribe. But they had their own trading in mind.

"They brought us to Najih that night, promising shelter while they decided what to do. But Najih used us as free labor and Ekon . . ." Wu rolled her eyes and let out a scoff. "I thought it was a mistake. I snuck out of Najih's estate and went back to the Temple of Mulgrum, to Priest Josiah, to tell him what Najih had done—was doing!" Wu could still feel the priest's cold fingers clamping her jaw shut as he hauled her through the city back to Najih. She pounded her thigh with her fist. "It was not a mistake! Most of the orphans at Najih's estate were handed over by the temple."

With wet eyes, Madhu asked, "Wu, where are these satyr ruins?"

"Madhu," Wu pleaded, rising. "He's a magus!"

Madhu's head tilted back in offense. "So am I." She lifted the green bag dangling from her belt and bounced it in the palm of her hand. "My community claims I'm one of the most gifted polyglot summoners they've had in generations, and I say we get your father's spear back." She withdrew from the fear on Wu's face then set her jaw. Her hand slapped against Wu's arm and gripped tightly. With a shake, Madhu insisted, "No. That spear belongs to your tribe—it belongs to you, Wu! We are doing this."

"Oui. Mais, we do not even know if the slavers are still there. The ghost may have fled by now."

"Then what have we to lose?" Madhu fell back against the post and perused her shirt's offerings. "We eat. Then we leave."

Chapter 6: Sneak Thieves

Swallowing the last bite of her flatbread, Wu studied Madhu's determination. It hadn't waned in the least as they had hurriedly started eating, Wu nervously devouring everything she touched. Hope of holding her father's spear again had begun to overtake her arguments against bringing her revenge to the Ghost and his slavers. "Are you sure you could match his magics, Madhu?"

Madhu waved Wu's concern aside. "In this region, he's probably just a hedge witch." Then she squinted and thought. "I suppose he may have more experience. But someone like that must pay for what they do to others, Wu!"

"Certainly, I agree . . ." But from just the two of them? Involving Madhu's caravan in the affair would not garner any support from the town's citizens. "Perhaps if we find my father's spear, Kruispad will treat me as the leader of a tribe. They could not possibly expect me to serve Najih. The Daijon are not greatly respected here, yet Anzante's sheikh has laws around our treatment that even Kruispad must obey." She knew that to be true by the fact that Rafit had his own stall and license to sell, not that he looked at all Creb. "And when Ekon and I are free, we can head north to where they will not turn a blind eye to slavery."

Honestly, she wasn't sure of that. After all, every traveler to Anzante knew to avoid lands near the borders for fear of the slavers. The sheikh had to have heard those rumors for himself and had never sent patrols to drive the slavers out that she had heard tale of. Her eyes lowered to her bandaged hand until Madhu covered it with her own.

"Then we steal back your spear," Madhu said. "Quietly. Like baru'baru—sneak thieves in the jungle." She nodded until Wu did. "Good. If nothing else, I promise to get you free of this place, Wu. You and your Ekon. You have my word as a Tabari. Bapu will relay this Ghost's whereabouts to the sheikh and explain to him our people will not trade with slaver countries. At the very least."

"It is not far from here," Wu said. "Eight miles? Southwest, past the date palm groves. We could be there within a few hours."

Madhu's playful grin returned. "Then we go tonight. I will borrow Babhru. If he's strong enough to run with Bapu riding him, he's strong enough for both of us."

Less amenable to riding, Wu frowned but nodded. "Najih may send someone to find me soon. Ekon may insist." She spotted her baskets by the caravan across the river. "I should go pick the olives and sneak out to rendezvous tonight."

"Why?" Madhu asked. "So he can cut you? No. You come with me. We will tell Bapu you had to run out earlier because you might have dysentery."

Wu grimaced. "Must we?"

With a twinkle of mischief in her eye, Madhu replied, "Yes. It's an easy thing to cure with our medicines. Then he won't mind us resting in the tent today."

Wu's conviction warred again with her nerves.

Madhu let out a frustrated, "Ahyee." She bumped Wu's arm as she passed. "Trust me."

With her hands over her belly to help sell the lie, Wu followed Madhu back to the caravan. Madhu's father had finished his meal as well. Within earshot, his Racinian guest perused the ground herbs and strange medicines in an opened babul wood cart. Wu blocked her view of the silver-mantled woman with Raza and adopted a pitiful look as she lowered her gaze to the man's jewel-buckled slippers.

The lie delivered, Madhu escorted Wu away from her father and into the chieftain's tent with his blessing and well-wishes. Wu feared it would be the first of many offenses committed against the Tabari before the night was through. She ran back to collect the stave from her baskets before returning to Madhu.

The tent Madhu shared with her father was as large as the dining tent, with Madhu's own area draped off for privacy. Incense filled the air, and everything had a pink hue thanks to the sunlight coming through the red fabric.

Following Madhu's lead, Wu kicked off her sandals and entered the pillow-padded tent.

"Help me prepare for tonight," Madhu said. She pointed to a small wooden chest of drawers in her nook. "Bring that over to the table, and I will compose my spells."

Heavier than Wu expected, the chest of eight square drawers clanged its metal rings as she wobbled with it over to the table Madhu had cleared and wiped clean.

Madhu removed the bottom two drawers completely and reached back into the chest to pull out a thick, dried stalk. "While I pestle the ruta stalk, would you mind grabbing my aga'lagi?"

Wu stepped back and eyed Madhu's mats and blankets. "Your what?"

"Behind my pillows. It's a jack wood stick with silk tacked to it at both ends." Groaning, Madhu strained at grinding the ruta stalk with the pestle.

Searching through the colorful silk pillows lining the side of Madhu's mats, Wu found it. Wavy fire symbols had been etched into the surface of the red wood slightly longer than a yard. Petal-shaped pieces of silk dangled from the ends. Held by a single tack each, the dark green and pale pink silks fluttered as Wu gave it a twirl.

Red sand and some herbs had been added to Madhu's mixture when Wu returned. She took the aga'lagi from Wu and said, "Green, I think." Gathering the green silk pieces together, she formed a bud-like shape. After stuffing the concoction into it, she tied it off with a single thread bound several times around the top.

Madhu frowned at what remained in her mortar. "That's not enough for anything." She dumped it out on the table. From the left drawer in the second row, she selected five dry brown leaves. "While I get more ruta, will you pestle this and then shave grass?" Once Madhu had added the thin green blades, she backed away for Wu to work. "It will make a paste."

Worried for her inexperience with magic, Wu worked the pestle hard, hoping she didn't disappoint Madhu and ruin her spell.

Within a few minutes, Madhu returned, shaking her hand in the air. She rubbed the thumb of her right hand. "Ahyee. Age has not dulled Karishma's keen ears or her aim."

"Should we ask her to join us?" Wu teased. "No more ruta then?"

Madhu shook her head. "We have enough for one. That should be plenty." To Wu's concern, she said, "We agreed to sneak in, remember? We shouldn't need it at all."

Her fingers pinched the remains from her last spell from the table and mashed them into the paste Wu had created. "I hope you're not afraid of snakes."

Wu flinched back. "Pourquoi?"

Madhu giggled. "You'll see. Or maybe you won't, if we're lucky." She mounded the paste onto the end of the stick as Wu helped her form the pink silk bud around it. Madhu gave it a satisfied nod and returned it to the pillow blockade.

Pointing at the pouches dangling from the gold silk cords tied about Madhu's waist, Wu asked, "What do those do?"

Madhu rolled her eyes. "Nothing helpful. But we're going to fix that." She removed all three and set them aside. From the chest of drawers, she pulled out another green pouch and a red one.

When they were filled, again with a wait-and-see explanation given for their functions, Wu helped to hide the evidence of their plans and to replace the components by the mortar with medicines the Tabari used for dysentery.

"Did you really have to use dysentery as the reason?"

"Yes," Madhu answered. "Bapu fears it more than bees. He may even spend the evening in Haani's tent."

Illusion prepared, they played games with hand-painted cards. When the fortune-telling deck Madhu used didn't propose positive outcomes for their adventure, she gathered up the deck and threw it into the tent wall.

As she set up a notched board and laid out colorful stones in its divots, Wu asked, "Madhu, where is your mother?"

"Back home. She couldn't come because she is with child." She paused and thought for a moment. "I think I am a sister now. Do you . . ." More somberly, she continued, "Did you have any brothers or sisters?"

Wu shook her head. She lay back on Madhu's mats and stared up into the blue sky through the small angled gaps on the ceiling's fabric. "We should rest, Madhu. No more games." That evening promised answers Wu wasn't sure she wanted. After all, if her mother had survived, she would have come for her. She pushed those thoughts out of her mind and enjoyed the sensation of safety. It had been so long since she had fallen asleep without fear of what might wake her.

As it turned out, it was Raza's murmuring voice. "Daughter," he whispered again.

Wu nudged Madhu awake. Stars appeared in the darkness through the gaps in the ceiling.

"Aye, yes, Bapu," she managed, rubbing her eyes.

Raza had not even entered his tent. His voice came through the doorway. "Is Wu feeling better?"

Madhu grinned victoriously. "Yes, Bapu. Some."

"Good, good. I will stay with Haani tonight. You may rest here."

"Good night, Bapu!"

"Good night, Daughter. Good night, Wu. I hope the morning brings peace to your body and mind."

Weakly, Wu replied, "Merci, Raza." Sitting up, Wu threw Madhu a frown, killing her friend's smile.

Madhu swatted her arm. She whispered, "You worry a lot for someone who sneaks out at night just to eat every day." She took up her aga'lagi, stood, and stretched. "How late is it?" After climbing onto the table, she spied through the flaps of the roof. "Good. The men have come out to buy what they don't want others to know they need."

Wu wasn't sure what that meant. Shortly into Madhu's explanation, she raised her hand to stop her.

After a giggle, Madhu said, "Bapu will be working for a short time still. I will grab some roti and whatever is left over from the feast. Maybe some mangoes. We can eat, then we go."

Devouring the delicious mint-and-coriander chutney, bread, and meat Madhu brought, Wu put her doubts to rest and built up her excitement. No longer would she be surviving, merely wondering what happened to her mother and her tribe, wondering how to break Ekon free of Najih's grasp. She would have answers. Even if the Ghost had carried his evils elsewhere, she would know and would have finally taken some action to save Ekon. And if all went according to Madhu's proclamations, her father's spear would find its way home to her grip.

On her toes, Madhu peeped out of the tent from the table again. She nodded to Wu with a smile and hopped down.

They crept through the tunnels between the tents, out into the spring backs' grassy pen, and straight to Babhru. The russet beast thrust his ivory horns into the air with a grunt as he inspected Wu.

Madhu unwound Babhru's long lead and whispered, "Let him smell your hand."

Babhru's head rose higher when Wu raised her palm up to him. She froze. Finally, he lowered his muzzle to sniff her several times. Wu hadn't expected much to happen. But when the spring back simply returned to grazing, Madhu wore a proud smile.

"Ohyee!" she whispered triumphantly. "He likes you!" Then she handed over his lead. "Take him out of the pen and start walking south. I will grab his saddle and catch up."

"Take him?" Wu asked.

She worried needlessly. As though he understood Madhu's wishes, Babhru walked himself to the gate and waited for Wu to open it. When she did, he passed through and waited for her to close it.

"You are very well behaved, Babhru. I suppose after such a long life, you must know quite a bit of Common, oui?" He didn't give an answer. She felt foolish for anticipating one and started their walk south, giving the caravan a wide berth.

If she felt silly for expecting a conversation with Babhru, Madhu looked it. Trailing through the tall grasses away from the city, petite Madhu carried her aga'lagi in one hand and steadied a large saddle on her hunched back with the other.

Wu stopped and brought Babhru back a short distance to greet her.

It took both of them to get the saddle situated on Babhru's tall back and both of them to get each other mounted.

With their staffs safely tucked into the saddle straps, Madhu asked, "Are you ready?"

Babhru looked back at them as Wu fidgeted to maintain her balance.

When she nodded, Madhu gave Babhru a kick.

Wu hugged Madhu tightly as the spring back raced forward. In under a minute, they had reached Najih's olive grove. In under five, they were breezing through the tall date palms on their way to the encroaching southern dunes. Slowly, Wu grew comfortable with the rhythm and sway of the warm beast. Her hands guided Madhu's to the west. "Stay in this direction. There are woods close to the ruins. We must stop there."

The desert sands didn't slow Babhru's wide hooves as Madhu guided him from patch of grassland to patch of grassland.

Just as Wu recalled, the sand became more plentiful. When it seemed they had finally left the river's touch, they crested a short ridge. The woods she remembered awaited them below.

Riding down into the sandy soil of the dying woods, Wu was surprised by how much two years had taken its toll. She carefully climbed out of Babhru's saddle before the spring back had fully stopped. "He should be safe here."

While patting Babhru's neck, Madhu scanned the scattered brush across the desiccated soil. The woods were shrinking into yet another small oasis.

"Tamarind?" Madhu asked of the tree before them. She slid off the saddle and loosely bound the spring back to it. "Do you think the river use to run through here?"

Wu threw her a puzzled look.

"The rivers move," Madhu explained. "Over time. I bet it ran through here in the time of the satyrs."

"We are not fortunate enough to have it or the satyrs with us now," Wu replied. She raised the end of her staff and pointed southwest. "Let us see what remains of the Ghost's haunt."

Chapter 7: The Ghost

From within the woods, they spied over a fallen tree to the satyr ruins. Fallen branches had been nailed together to form a rickety barricade around them. Doubts returned to Wu, but her feet moved forward without hesitation to the sand mounded about another dead tree at the edge of the oasis. Soon, she would have answers to the questions she had tried to ignore for years.

The full moon shone down over speared skulls crenellating the ugly fence about the ruins. Wu forced herself to study them for familiarity. But she couldn't identify any of them. Most had lost their flesh long ago.

Perhaps Madhu had been right about the river. Minarets encircled by heavy stone vines and flowers stood over the domed structures and dated the ruins to a time when jungles reigned over these parts of Anzante. Grand cockatrices topped the minarets. Their widespread wings and serpentine tails had cracked, worn down by the wind and the sun.

Madhu appeared at Wu's side. "Ahyee," she said in disgust for the heads. "Barbaric and unclean. This Ghost deserves to know what awaits him through the veil."

They both jumped when a distant drumbeat struck. Others followed, slower in pace than Wu's heart. Distant cheers erupted.

"Someone is home," Madhu said.

Wu agreed. "He has visitors." She directed Madhu's attention to a series of crude canvas tents on this side of the fence at the northern end of the old town.

Taking Wu's wrist, Madhu brought her under the empty gazes of the Ghost's victims and to the northeast side of the fence. They trespassed through the warning and hid behind an empty slave cart enclosed with rusty iron bars. Wind had mounded sand around everything stationary, which did not include the line of carts.

Looking out through the fence, Wu noticed two servants in tattered long tunics tending mounts by the tents. Peering into the ancient town between the satyrs' rotund buildings, Wu spotted nothing alive. The ancient marketplace appeared as deserted as the night she'd escaped.

The drums' dirge was the only sign of life. "Be careful," Wu said. "There are catacombs under the ruins, and the satyrs' stones do not hold as well as dwarves'." She pointed to the large hole near the Temple of Maris where it had collapsed. Squinting, she tried to determine if that was where she and Ekon had escaped. Some of the details from that night weren't as clear as others.

For a brief moment, she wondered if her mother was still down there. She knew in her heart she wasn't. Her mother hadn't been down there for years. The short-lived hope stung.

"I do not see any guards," Madhu said, stepping out into the open.

Wu muttered, "Guards are for those who fear."

With a watchful eye on the servants tending the steeds, they raced into the desecrated Temple of Maris. The destruction had worsened to include chiseled profanity in the deity's side and more than one person had urinated in there.

"Hooha." Madhu groaned at the smell. "I do not follow these gods, but I would never be so rude to one. They are bold." She went to Maris's broken idol. "We will seek vengeance on your behalf as well."

Spying through the doorway, Wu studied the temples and collapsing estates lining the forum and the ancient marketplace. They appeared deserted. "The drums are that way," she said, pointing through the wall of the temple to the southwest. "Should we see what they are doing?"

As they passed the hole to the slave pits, Wu noted it had been planked over from underneath. Still half-tempted to retrace her steps from that night, she let the notion go. The Ghost had been excited when he had discovered the magic in her father's spear; he would not leave such a find to a dungeon's decay. The symbol of her tribe didn't linger down there any more than her mother's hibiscus scent.

The slavers had made their own market for trade among themselves. Where the forum met the marketplace, tattered fabrics hung from wooden frames. No wares had been left unattended. Naturally. Their clientele were the lowest of thieves. The only things safe from their sticky fingers were the empty amphorae under centuries of dust in cluttered corners.

Crouched low, Wu followed Madhu in the shadows of the masonry counters along the stall fronts of the long macellum where the satyrs once peddled their wares.

Madhu tittered more than once for the abundance of phalluses decorating the satyrs' old thermopolia and either side of every entry they passed.

As they neared the end of the market, muttering, angry voices reached them.

They slowed and cut between buildings to get away from the main thoroughfare. A gang of servants waited at the edge of a sunken amphitheatre, partially listening and occasionally uttering complaints about their trek through the desert and how far inland they had had to ride. Long daggers on each of their hips said they voluntarily served their slaver masters. The weapons also sped Wu's heartbeat to where she barely heard the drums.

She tapped two fingers to Madhu's shoulder and pointed to a squat domed structure to their right. Taking the lead, she crept lowly across the grit. Her breathing only fully returned to her when she and Madhu reached the backside of the turf-and-travertine hut repurposed to store hay. After passing her staff to Madhu, she scaled the disjointed blocks carefully, though it was an easier climb than Najih's tower. Somewhat satisfied with her perch on the crumbling curved roof, she reached down for her staff and Madhu's aga'lagi. When Madhu crouched at her side, they scooted around, flattened across the dome, and spied down into the amphitheatre.

Slavers dotted the tiered semicircle of seats. Vetskarran roughs, a handful of Tazzarians in their golden robes and strange censer-like necklaces, and others who appeared to be Anzantean lords dressed in colorful silk jibbas watched a lineup of slaves at the base of the bowl. Some were Daijon. Some appeared to be unlucky travelers; one, a pale fat man. But Wu's attention swept past them and straight to the man from her nightmares.

Centered between his servants beating their goblet drums, the Ghost set their rhythm by stabbing the air overhead with her father's spear. White paint covered the dark skin of his face and bare arms. He wore a bone necklace that looked distinctly like human ribs and smaller bones in bracelets around his wrists and both ankles.

Wu rolled onto her back, her resolve evaporating, leaving tendrils of cold creeping through her chest. She put her right hand to her heart and whispered, "That is him. With my father's spear." Her eyes leaked tears at their corners. What defilement had it suffered in the man's hands?

"Him?" Madhu asked in disbelief. "He's scrawny, Wu. A long-boned, scrawny man who paints himself to hide how pathetic a creature the gods made him to be."

Wu shot her an incredulous look. "Can you not sense the dark magics the man weaves at a whim? His evil?"

Shrugging, Madhu said, "It is just magic. I'm more afraid of the manticore than your Ghost. You didn't tell me about that."

Manticore? Wu turned back onto her belly.

Elephant-gray and elephant-sized, a lionlike beast stood alert but eerily still in the depth of the amphitheatre. Its leathery wings were tucked close to its sides under the thick-shelled scorpion tail arching over its back. Around its neck, orange glyphs shone through its iron collar.

When Wu realized only the feeble and wounded awaited purchase in the manacled line, her heart sank. Silence fell over the amphitheatre.

"My colleagues," the Ghost called out in Common. "Welcome to Paradise!"

"Ya-hah!" the Vetskarrans cheered, causing Wu to flinch.

The Ghost shook the bones on his arms and stamped his feet in celebration. "It may not look like the oasis you dream of. But here, the only laws are mine." Many of the slavers laughed. "And the prices the cheapest you'll find in this desert." He hopped down and walked the line before his prisoners. "I have decided to give you a show to whet your appetites and start your visit on the right foot."

He looked up and down the line and grinned widely for his audience. "If any of these slaves appeal to you, I suggest you bid on them now."

The crowd laughed.

Madhu raised her aga'lagi.

"No," Wu pleaded. "There are too many of them. We could never . . ."

Angry at first, Madhu stared at her. Then she closed her eyes and lowered her weapon.

The Ghost's prisoners began to whimper, save for one. Sandy and ashen from their long imprisonment, the old Daijon man stood straight-backed to make eye contact with every one of the slavers. One strand of thick orange beads hung intact amid the broken strings dangling from his necklace.

"I won't beg!" the old man yelled in her parents' tongue. He took the hand of the elderly woman next to him. "I have seen your souls! In the next life, you will suffer! For the gods know your deeds!"

The Ghost loosed a hearty laugh that echoed. He shouted, "Tell your gods we are coming for them next." He pointed a finger at the manticore, vanquishing the glow from its collar.

The beast shook its black mane and built a thunderous growl in its throat as it came to, its feral gaze fixed on the Ghost. A quiet vibration erupted into a roar. Venom glistened on the tip of its tail. Scraping metal on stone captivated the manticore, drawing its attention to one of the Ghost's servants. He ran down the line of captives, dragging a pair of manacles on the ground behind him, then slung them. They clattered to the feet of the elderly couple. The beast pounced.

On her back, Wu stared at the stars through the screams and chewed her bottom lip. Was this what had become of Gbad'Turu? Gentle Gbad'Evarie? Were these the drums she and Ekon had heard?

Madhu watched the spectacle with a disbelieving frown, soon replaced with a pout between her wet cheeks.

When the screams and cheering had ended, Wu quietly said, "Madhu, let us go. We have our lives. I will find another way to free Ekon."

"'Our lives'?" she asked as though it were a ridiculous consideration.

"Enjoy!" the Ghost yelled to grand applause.

Suddenly, Madhu crouched on the lip of the roof and warily watched the road from the amphitheatre to the marketplace.

The Ghost led a dozen of his servants down the road. The Gbad spear pointed their way.

To be close enough to see the whiskers on the man's face sent shivers through Wu. She grabbed Madhu's hand. But her Tabari friend dropped down to spy. Wu had little choice but to follow.

The Ghost and his faithful, each armed with sword or scimitar, marched proudly to the true entry of the catacombs in the east, between the holy forum and marketplace.

She and Madhu sidled around the round buildings as the slavers emerged from the amphitheatre. More often than not, Wu simply returned Madhu's dazed stared, sharing their horror through expression alone.

Finally, when they were convinced the guests had gathered in their tents, Madhu said, "We're not giving up, but we must be wise."

"This doesn't feel wise." Wu's eyeline drifted to the carnage in the amphitheatre, mercifully blocked by the building they had climbed.

"Be brave, Gbad'Wu. Nowhere on the lengthy list of what that man deserves will you find your tribe's spear. Nothing sacred. And no prosperity." She peered out into the marketplace with the green bud of her aga'lagi poised near her lips.

Deftly, they skirted the path the Ghost had taken. Drunken shouts and laughter muffled the women's cries for help from the tents. Wu tightened her grip on her staff and fed her anger without putting words to her fears.

Braving the open expanse, they ran to the stairs leading down to the catacombs and squinted to see inside. As Wu stared into the darkness, a thought occurred to her. If they vanished tonight, no one, neither Raza nor Ekon, would know how or why. She kept the realization to herself. Hoping Ekon would forgive her for undoing her rescue from that night, Wu stepped forward to linger at the entrance, not yet ready to admit she could not help those women in the tents.

The Ghost did this to them. He must pay.

Madhu took her by the hand and brought her deeper into his realm.

Chapter 8: The Fallen

Hiding away from the sun, the Ghost had created a lavish underground sanctuary tiled in marble and embellished with flaking gold leaf. Notably, his dwelling was not far enough away to avoid the cries from his prisoners in the pits. The familiar wailing froze Wu in place, standing in the deep shadow where an off-shooting, dank tunnel led to the captives. How many Daijon had fallen victim to him? How many of her people were left?

With a nudge, Madhu got her moving again.

But her heart stopped her. "No, Madhu," she whispered and doubled back to sneak down the decrepit tunnel. The scuffle of her sandals, the smell of the dirt, and her own heartbeat inhibiting her hearing fed the cold in her digits and the tears in her eyes. "We must help them, if we can. They're more important . . ."

Remembering where the guards had taken their posts as she and her tribe were separated and caged, Wu hugged the wall and sidled closer to the eight doorways at the tunnel's end. Hefty oil lamps kept the corridor lit brightly and the pit chambers dim. She glanced down to her thin staff and wished she had stolen a blade from one of the Kruispad stalls before they'd left. "Do you have a spell to kill the guards?"

Madhu's face waned at the question. "I do. But . . . we need them for him."

Ducking her head in thought, Wu decided she would have to be fast enough to keep them quiet. She could do this. She was not unarmed. "Wait here."

"Wu?" Madhu waited for her full attention. "Are you sure?"

"I would dishonor my tribe if I did not try to save these people."

Reaching to her belt, Madhu selected the red bag. She untied it from the golden cord and held it close to her chest before she urged Wu on with a nod.

Lightly stepping, Wu edged her way alone to the corner of the first arched opening on her left, with her gaze stuck to the one on her right. The corridor reeked of fear, waste, and death. She peered around into the archway. Broken amphorae filled the corners of the room where a metal grate lay over the hole in its center. The guard wasn't there.

Just as she began crossing to the other side of the corridor, a young man exited the last archway on the left.

Wu froze.

He spotted her immediately and drew his long scimitar. "Ghezo, one has escaped!"

A second man with a simple spear emerged from the right.

Just as Wu had readied her staff and taken a step back, a gust pressed her forward.

Halfway to her, the guards coughed. Unable to stop, they bent over and gasped for air. The one with the spear collapsed. Blood trickled from his lips, yet he still convulsed and looked to his cohort for help. A clicking hum coming from the man's chest sped into a buzz. Confused, he finally fell dead.

Hacking with his back against the wall, the live guard's eyes bulged further when a red-and-green ringed wasp crawled out of the fallen guard's mouth and inspected the blood running down his chin. Veins protruded and pulsed across the guard's face. The dying man fell to all fours scowling up at Wu. He tried to scream until more insects filled his mouth and nostrils. With a final jerk, he met his demise.

Wu searched behind her for Madhu.

Coming forward from the tunnel, Madhu whispered, "Lung-eater hornets. Keep your mouth closed. They will disappear in a moment." She drew Wu back a few more steps.

They huddled together and waited for the buzzing to pass. That close, Wu could feel Madhu trembling. She gave her a questioning glance.

"I have never used magic as a weapon before," she explained. "I know they were cruel . . . evil, but . . ." She shook her head. "No! I will protect you. Be it on them. Be it all on them." As she sneered at the bodies, the hornets vanished.

Cautiously, Wu moved farther in while Madhu examined the guards. No other guards awaited them in the remaining rooms. She went into the final chamber on the left and glanced up to the ceiling at the wooden planks sealing the hole she and Ekon had used in their escape. This was where her father had died. She clenched her side and breathed deeply.

"Who are you?" a man asked. His brown eyes bobbed in and out of view beneath the grate covering the pit.

Kneeling next to the hole, Wu slid into her Daijon tongue. "Do not worry. We will get you out of there." She could not see very well into the shadows yet but made out four forms below. They shuffled as they rose. "I am Gbad'Wu."

"Gbad?" another man asked. "Is Gbad'Wole here?"

Wu closed her eyes upon hearing her father's name and controlled her breathing. "I—no. Give us a moment. We will free you."

"My wife!" one of the prisoners yelled loudly enough to echo. "Is she there? In the other room? The guards took her."

Rushing into the room, Madhu hushed the man below with a lowered hand. "What?" she asked Wu.

Wu translated. "His wife was taken. He asked if she was in the other rooms." To the man, she said, "We will look."

Madhu pulled up the gold pouch from her belt and opened it. To Wu's surprise, it held a small metal dish and a candlenut. With a tap of her fingernail, fire roasted the nut in a slow, steady flame, giving off enough light to coat the floor around them and to see the worried faces below.

They began inspecting the room across the corridor.

Wu whispered, "Did the guards have the keys?"

Madhu nodded and glanced into the pit in the center of the room. Empty. As was the third. The fourth contained children, which they would need the men to help free. Wu calmed them as best she could and promised to return shortly.

As Madhu brought light into the fifth prison chamber, Wu's knees went weak. Colorful beads, many stained with blood, had been scattered to the far edges of the room, mounded against the remains of the amphorae. Human bones filled the pit halfway up to the grate.

One bead caught Wu's eye. Thick and long, the pale blue tube had not evaded the bloodstains either. She fell to her knees and snatched it up, then grabbed a bright purple one nearby. Another blue. She filled her hands, sniveling as she gathered them.

"What are you doing?" Madhu asked.

"Blue and purple hibiscus," Wu managed. She sniffed and swallowed the bitterness. "They grew along the streams we often followed in our travels through the plains. When one had begun to wilt, my mother would pluck it and wear it behind her ear." Now left to the rats, her beads had been scattered, mixed with strangers', dragged behind the old amphorae. Unidentifiable. "That is why my father chose these colors for the necklace he gave her. I know it by heart." Wu's eyes refused to stop scanning the scattered beads until she spotted the soft yellow of Gbad'Zoya's necklace and began gathering those as well.

"Here," Madhu said, presenting her empty red spell bag. "Put them in here." She helped Wu collect what they could find.

Though Wu knew there were more somewhere on the sticky floor, she let Madhu tie off the bag. She placed it in Wu's hand and closed her fingers around it.

Glancing back to the corridor, Madhu whispered, "Wu, that man's wife is likely the one we heard crying out . . . If we let them go, they will draw attention."

Wu shook her head and forced the bag of beads securely behind her belt. "You are smart, Madhu, and kind; but you do not know the Daijon." She rose and peered down into the pit and the mounds of bones that likely contained more than one person she held dear. "Someday, I will return and lay them to rest properly." She wiped her face, kissed her fingertips, and touched the bag of beads. Then she held her palm out for the keys to the pit.

After hesitating with a deep breath, Madhu handed them over.

More beads flooded the final room they searched. Only the men and the children remained to be sold.

Wu returned to the captives in the pit that had once held her, jabbed the key into the rusted iron lock, and twisted it off. She and Madhu lifted the metal grate up on its shrill hinges and laid it to rest against the wall.

A healthy man nearing his middle years was the first to be raised to freedom. "Did you find her?" he asked.

Wu pointed her finger to the ceiling. "We think the slavers have her in their tents."

Madhu flung her an incredulous look, correctly guessing what she had said.

Though anger bordered his dark features, the man said, "You have my thanks."

"Brother," the second man out said, "gather what weapons you can. We will free her first." As the worried husband went about doing as instructed, the younger one came to Wu. "Gbad'Wu, I am Jomo'Kar. You have my thanks and that of the Jomo tribe." His eyes flickered Madhu's way. "How many of your tribe are here?"

Wu bowed her head. "Me. I think." After finding the beads, she knew it to be true. But she wouldn't say it aloud. "My friend Madhu is helping me recover my father's spear. Does the Ghost have your relic?"

"The Ghost?" Jomo'Kar shook his head. "We hid it. After hearing the Gbad tribe and many others had gone missing when seeking a cure to the creeping death, we did not dare risk it."

"There are children here," Wu said. "Come."

The man returned with the guards' weapons and joined them to help release the young ones. The children buried their terrified faces against the chests of the men as they were swept up into hugs. Reunited with their tribe, the children did exactly as they were told.

Jomo'Kar received the guard's scimitar.

The spear went to one of the other two men, who then said, "Brother."

Nodding, Jomo'Kar took the lead, hunkering down to begin the hunt as Wu's father had so many times. Everyone followed behind him to the exit.

Then, when they were spying out to the open expanse of the forum and the slavers' tents to the north, Madhu warned, "If you fight them, you will die."

Jomo'Kar set his jaw and said in Common, "We are Daijon hunters, little one. Those men will never see us coming." He gestured for his men to begin the hunt outside. One escorted the children out, as quiet as a breeze. Staring down the path to the Ghost and his guard, Jomo'Kar said, "When we are finished, we will help you with this witch."

"No!" Wu said. "Go. Get away. Save your relic and your tribe. Spread word through the north. Warn others not to come here! Tell them what has happened." Wu straightened her back at the man's unsure expression. "Promise me you will do this. It is more important. More important than the

Gbad tribe." The statement stung and brought tears to her eyes.

With an admiring gaze, Jomo'Kar said, "From tribe leader to tribe leader." He patted his fist to his chest twice. "You have my word and my gratitude, Gbad'Wu. Know this, Cousin; if you and any of your tribe wish to join the Jomo, we welcome you always."

Unable to stop herself, Wu threw her arms around his torso and squeezed tightly. He patted her back and held her close.

"Brother," a voice beckoned from outside.

Jomo'Kar released her and smiled. "I pray for Gbad'Wole to lend us his skill."

Wu watched them go. "May the gods beat the drums in your favor." Once the Jomo had disappeared into the shadows of the old marketplace, Wu clenched her staff and said in Common to Madhu, "The Gbad tribe is not dead. We are here, and I will prove it." She set off into the Ghost's domain.

Chapter 9: Farewell

Deeper into the Ghost's lair, Wu realized she had been mistaken. The Ghost hadn't built these ornate halls; the satyrs had. She had never heard of the extinct race living underground, but the cracked frescos depicted their gatherings in great forests with elves and humans. Gathered without cavorting. No fauns at play. Dressed for war? Their bearded faces were somber.

Wu and Madhu crept into a long room of columns surrounding a dilapidated fountain, now a stagnant pool whose water had been tinged to a thick olive green. The stench of death continued down here, just when Wu had believed her nostrils clear of it. Reliefs of rustling leaves outlined sixteen empty floor-to-ceiling alcoves that suggested the room had been built for a grander purpose than displaying cobwebs and dirt. Certainly grander than the short, cylindrical oil lamps housed in the alcoves now. Each lamp had a ghost-white symbol, perhaps a rune, painted on the front of it. Wu kept her distance from both the symbols and the cesspool's tainted water.

Voices could be heard farther in. Someone scuffled about in an adjoining hallway. The sound of clinking dishes came from another. But they didn't deter Wu. She knew exactly where they should continue their search. To the right of the pool, flanking an archway, chiseled black stone formed two tall nude women wearing gold belts and nothing else. They flanked an archway to a room the satyrs must have used for something sacred, as the detailed friezes of grapes and leaves, now broken to fit in the nude women, spread halfway to the alcoves on either side.

Slowly making their way from column to column and past the one hallway opening they had to cross, they reached the Ghost's treasury. A round table ten feet wide held so many weapons it made Wu weak. A pair of red steel war hammers. A golden dagger. Three black steel swords of differing designs. Those she knew to be Daijon. She put her hand over her heart, trying to discern how many others belonged to tribes now lost. A long gap in the center of the table split the stolen hoard, just long enough for her father's spear.

Feeling as a horse in the clouds must, she scanned the room in hopes they could retrieve the spear and leave immediately. But it was not to be. Books in various states of disrepair, hung tapestries with precious metal threads, dyed silks, even toppled piles of coins rested atop the furniture about the room. Yet there was no spear.

Searching, she went left to where a glass sarcophagus housed a headless skeleton. Wu moved closer to examine the black flecks covering the bones. Shiny beetles as large as her thumbnail wandered through crevices.

"They eat dead flesh," Madhu said. "That many . . . this could have been a body only hours ago."

Drawn to a strange glass bowl of dark liquid inset into the wall, Madhu approached it cautiously. "This feels . . . bad. Wrong. Slick and dirty." She shivered and took a step back.

As Wu neared, she covered her nose to block the smell of the fermented contents. The golden lid did little to contain the odor. "It smells worse." The water had grown darker and greener than that in the cesspool. Something floated against the glass. Fur? An animal? Wu squinted. Hair. She looked back at the glass sarcophagus. Frowning, she stepped away from the horror and looked to Madhu.

Distant voices came closer through the doorway. Wu and Madhu quickly hid under the massive table, crawling deep to its center. They put their backs to the stone pillar supporting it and watched.

Two men walked into the room, one in a jibba with a fraying hem and threadbare slippers, the other barefoot under his bone ankle bracelets. Long, yellow toenails ended the bony feet speckled with white paint. The black steel end of her father's spear dropped to the floor with each step of the magus's right foot. The dense pearwood weapon of the Gbad tribe lifted from her view before it slid atop the table over her.

"What brings you unbeckoned to my domain?" the Ghost asked.

"Ah, yes," the jibba-wearing man said. "While it is good that I visit the area on occasion—to keep the illusion of my grand find alive—this time . . . this time I wish to discuss my fee, Monsieur Roho."

The Ghost's feet turned away from him and wandered over to the strange bowl in the wall. "It has been a generous arrangement."

His tone disagreeing, the man said, "Yes. But you must see it from my perspective." He lifted something heavy from the table, then set it back down. Wu guessed it to be the golden dagger. "Seeing all of this . . . the scales are hardly balanced. Am I not the source of this wealth? I poison the flies. I send the flies to your web."

Poisoned them?

The Ghost cackled wildly, stirring the fine hairs on Wu's neck. "I see you, Banno Tuyu." He turned to face the man. "Those years ago, when I came to you, I came to a handsome man, a charming man who could tell you the rain fell from the sun, and you would believe it. A man who would never poison or lie to the innocent." He closed the space between them. "Now, I see a man with many chins. Thin hair. A sad, wrinkled face. Greed on your lips. I see you, Banno Tuyu. And I must make a change."

Blood spattered across the floor.

Madhu and Wu joined hands.

Banno fell to his knees clutching his throat and collapsed before them. He spoke in croaking gasps. When his eyes focused on them, they bulged wider. His blood flowed, forcing Wu and Madhu back.

Madhu rounded the stone pillar supporting the table, but Wu stared him in the eye. Yes. She had seen this pudgy face and thinly shaved beard before. In Pulasa, this man had told her father of the supposed cure in the satyr ruins.

The Ghost kicked the dying man in the side. "There are plenty younger and prettier than you who will poison and peddle my tales to Daijon for what I am willing to pay." He called for his servants.

Wu joined Madhu on the opposite side of the pillar.

Two pairs of ashen feet in sandals appeared in the doorway.

"My beetles have finished their meal," the Ghost said. "Add her bones to the others."

Their robes dipped to the floor as they bowed. "Do you wish us to feed him to your beetles, my master?"

The Ghost scoffed in disgust. "You believe his face is worthy of my chalice?" He spit on the floor. "Imbecile." A silence lingered. "No. Feed Banno to the manticore. She is with child. The fat will do her good." He laughed.

Wu clutched her staff with both hands when the servants grabbed the dead liar's arms and legs. But they did not notice her and Madhu. The fat man slowly lifted out of view and dripped blood in a trail through the door.

The Ghost swayed and hummed, mumbling words to himself, as he glided back to his "chalice." Wu heard his finger tapping the glass.

Madhu nudged Wu and nodded with a question in her eye. When Wu nodded back, Madhu brought the green silk bud at the end of her staff close to her lips. She whispered, "Membatu dan mengikat." An orange swirling light trickled out of the bud and rode the air over the spilled blood toward the Ghost. It tapped the Ghost's calf and coated the man in a flash.

Climbing out from under the table, Wu studied the unmoving man.

Like oil spilled in a puddle, whirling orange and yellow patterns cocooned him as they drifted about his body.

"Wu," Madhu whispered from across the table. Her eyes fell to the Gbad spear. Then she scurried to the doorway.

Wu gently lifted her father's spear from the table and set her staff in its place. The Ghost had added a few nicks and scrapes to its pearwood shaft. She held the spear to her chest and closed her eyes. Her anger directed her closer to the Ghost, stone-still in the shifting light. Within a thought, she stood next to him, the murderer of her tribe. Vengeance in her heart guided her hand. Wu struck. But spear's point clinked against the orange aura.

"No!" Madhu yelled.

The spell vanished. Freed of the enchantment, the Ghost blinked in a daze. Then he noticed Wu beside him. His eyebrows rose in fury when he spotted the spear in her hands.

"Dam may liocabla!" Madhu commanded before her green pouch struck his chest. A dense cloud swarmed from the bag, holding his legs in place. "Wu!"

Wu fell back from the tendrils of mist reaching for her. With Madhu's pull, she got back to her feet.

Abruptly, the spell vanished. "I too know the power of magic," the Ghost said to Madhu. "Let me show you."

Just as suddenly, the mist reappeared. Reinvigorated, it snagged the Ghost's arms and pulled him down to his knees.

They ran, brushing past two guards in their flight.

"You will not escape me!" the Ghost howled. His laughter followed them past the pool and down the halls, never growing quieter. "My pets love little girls. So tender! Your marrow so juicy!"

Footsteps scraped after them, but Wu refused to slow to look back. She didn't even slow at the exit to the underground lair. Wu held her father's spear at the ready and charged ahead into the marketplace. Silence greeted them. Fires crackled unattended. A red scarf tumbled in the breeze.

A rattling growl turned them back to the lair. Four yellow eyes stared out from the shadows. Six more joined it.

Madhu seized Wu's wrist. "Varrows! Run!" They darted across the forum. "Their claws are venomous. Don't let them touch you," she yelled.

They needed a distraction. Wu hauled her straight along in the direction of the tents. They climbed over the fence, accidently dislodging the skulls. Jomo'Kar and his hunters had already laid waste to the slavers; their corpses lay in their blood across the mats and toppled tables. Wu suddenly regretted insisting the Jomo tribe move on without her and Madhu. Wu glanced back under the tent's canopy.

Under the moonlight, two purple-skinned varrows chased after them through the forum. Their rattling purr preceded them. Swinging the arced black blade at the end of their tails, they ducked their horned toad-like heads and charged.

Running through the dead slavers' mounts, Wu and Madhu reached the sand and sprinted for the unobstructed woods where Babhru waited. They'd never reach him in time. "There is nowhere to hide!" Wu said. "How do we stop them?" She checked behind her.

Her ploy had worked somewhat, distracting one of the varrows with the horses. The lead varrow hadn't taken the bait. Something had fought the terror before. The tall jagged spike atop its head had been broken. Two of the predator's yellow eyes had been gouged out.

"Only magic works," Madhu panted. "Magic spells. Magic weapons to pierce their oily hides." With a glance back at their impending hunter, Madhu stopped. She raised her aga'lagi and spoke into the pink silk bud. "Cuon dây mien phí!" A sparkling blue cloud burst forward and divided into three. The spell darkened, hissed, and thickened into a trio of winged king cobras.

Darting through the air directly for the varrow, the black snakes captivated the beast. One swing of the varrow's tail spike was all it managed before the snakes swooped around it. Constricting, they bit into its bumpy leathery hide and rode the dying beast to the ground, silencing its rattle.

The second varrow's bloodlust had finished off the horses. It leaped onto the camel. Still bound to the tent post, the camel groaned and bucked to shake the beast off. Though it nearly brought down the tent, it could not escape. The varrow's claws tore into the camel's side as it sank its teeth into the neck. The arched black blade of its tail punctured deep into the camel's gut and brought a quick end to its resistance.

"That was my last spell," Madhu whispered. She took Wu's hand as they backed away into the sands, careful not to draw a single yellow eye their way. When they were fifty yards away from the varrow's savage gluttony, they ran.

Once in the woods, Wu hid behind a dead tree and glanced back. The varrow was nowhere to be seen. "Will it follow us?"

"I don't know. Maybe. Varrows are voracious and smart but not very loyal." She shrugged an apology. "I don't know much more. Necromancy is only something we study to counter. But we must move, Wu."

"Necromancy?" Wu asked. She took two steps before she heard the rattling purr.

Leaping from the shadows, the varrow cleared her head in its path to Madhu. Its claws scratched across Madhu's back, splattering Wu's legs with blood. Madhu fell forward. The beast stood over her.

Releasing an enraged roar, Wu stabbed the varrow through its ribs. She forced the beast away from Madhu and down to the dirt as she had once seen her father do to a lioness. She didn't remove the spear until its double-pupiled eyes stilled.

Wu tore out the Gbad spear and held the blade away from her to keep the varrow's dark blood from dripping on her or Madhu. "Madhu!"

She didn't stir.

Setting the spear aside, Wu knelt and lifted Madhu's wrist to kiss the back of her hand. Her fingers smelled of mangoes. "Please, Madhu. Wake."

Chapter 10: The Monk, the Mage, and the Midwife

Madhu winced as she roused and whimpered. She fell silent again.

"Stay with me," Wu demanded.

Managing to get Madhu lying over her back, Wu took up her father's spear and walked hunched over, praying after every tree to find Babhru. Her legs burned, but she kept her pace, refusing to slow. Finally, she found the ruddy spring back.

He stopped chewing and watched her approach.

Wu paused when the creature bowed his head and knelt for her to lay Madhu across the saddle. "She is wounded," Wu said, untying his reins. "We must get her back quickly." That meant she needed to ride as well. She slid the Gbad spear and Madhu's aga'lagi through the saddle straps. In an uneasy balance, she mounted Babhru behind the saddle with one hand gripping the reins and the other stabilizing Madhu. She clicked her tongue.

Babhru sprang ahead, leaping faster and farther than he had in bringing them there. Wu struggled but stayed on his back by lying over Madhu as he bounded through the sand, through the date palms, and past the olive grove. Only amid the low-lit lanterns of the Tabari's tents did he slow. "Help!" Wu cried through her dry throat. Her voice cracked. "Help!" she shouted, stronger this time.

Babhru stopped the instant he saw Raza come out of the tents. The large, bearded man dashed to them and helped Madhu down. He paled at the blood on her back. "Daughter!" he called over the gasps and murmurs of the Tabari rushing to help. "Daughter! Madhu, dearest." He brought his daughter to the reed mats near their wares and examined her wounds.

Wu removed her spear and the aga'lagi from Babhru's saddle straps and followed. She passed Madhu's weapon to her father.

He received it and raised his brow. Accusations of foolishness tinged his question, "What did this?"

"A varrow," Wu answered.

The Tabari around them gasped and loosed ahyees.

"It is dead," Wu added quickly. "I killed it." She displayed the dark clumps of the creatures blood on her spearhead.

Raza relented. "But it will not save her. She is poisoned. There is no cure."

"There is," the old Racinian woman said, creeping up through the huddle behind Wu. Dressed in a simple blue robe and a long gray shawl, the woman had also bothered to don her silver mantle amid the spectacle. She pointed to a green single-person canvas tent between the bridge and the caravan and spoke to a young man behind Raza. "You look spry. Hurry now and bring my bag. The sackcloth one."

Parting the crowd with a fishtailing hand, she made her way to Madhu. Her fingers began carefully picking the shredded cloth out of Madhu's wounds. With the damp fabric cleared, Wu saw the welts the beast had left behind. The cuts were shallow, but the skin had swollen around them. The Racinian touched the purpling skin and hissed. She accepted a wet cloth from one of the women and began patting the area clean. "Her fever is high. We must hurry. Where is he?" She glanced up. "Ah."

The young man ran to her beckoning hand and delivered a hefty, half-filled burlap sack.

Rooting around, the woman clicked her tongue several times before removing a purple bundle. She unfolded it. Bright red berries still clung to their branches within. Picking them free, the Racinian said, "These grow abundantly in the northern parts of the continent and out in the archipelago." When she had a handful, she mashed them with her fingers. Then she rubbed the mush into Madhu's puffy wounds. "Rowan berries will not ease the sting, but they will counter the toxins and the swelling. The venom does not travel in the blood, merely attacks the broken flesh." Only when Madhu's back had been covered with a thick layer of the pulpy salve did the woman stop.

As two of the Tabari women bound the injuries with a clean linen dressing, Raza asked Wu, "What were you two doing that brought out a varrow?"

"That is not important to you," the Racinian said, wiping her fingers off on a rag. "Listen to me, Raza Rao." She pointed both hands at Madhu. "Your daughter must get to the Tower of Trône d'Argent as quickly as possible. They'll know what to do if those berries are not enough." She removed the silver mantle from her shoulders and handed it to him. "Hide this until you reach the gates at Verdict Hill. Present it to the guards and say, 'My daughter is ill. Mage Ailsa Briggs sent me to speak with Grand Diviner Sylvester.' Do this even after she regains her smile. You must be sure." The woman wore a mother's warning glare not to defy her.

"Bring Babhru," he said.

The travelers sprang into action, helping Raza into his saddle with Madhu, loading the spring back with rations and coin, and making promises of upholding responsibilities until they were rejoined. "We will send word to Rashmi and find you in Trône d'Argent," one of the men said. "Blessings be upon you, Raza."

Raza shifted with his daughter in his lap and squeezed Babhru's reins in his hand. "You have been a blessing on us, more than any guest should be, Mage Ailsa Briggs. The Tabari are eternally grateful, and we will remember your name."

Solemnly, the woman replied, "We saved her." She nodded Wu's direction before ducking her head and waving out her arm to the road.

Raza nodded his thanks to Wu and wore the kind smile in his white beard that she expected from him. Babhru sprang away.

Her eyes stung watching Madhu and Raza ride off to somewhere she could not follow. She did not even get to say goodbye. Or thank you. With this mage's insistence that Madhu go to Racine's Tower, could she even guess the true price Madhu would pay for her to reclaim her father's spear?

Misunderstanding Wu's questioning stare, Ailsa said, "She will live." The old woman stroked Wu's arm with her soft hand.

Wu sniffled, jerked away, and shot the woman a heated glare, earning herself a few cold stares from the Tabari.

"Mage Briggs," a woman whose hair was wrapped in red sheer silk said, "we must be on our way shortly. Can we offer you any food, wares—anything to comfort your travels? As Raza has said, we are ever grateful to you."

"Thank you, Aparna. I shall be setting out myself." She slung the sackcloth bag over her shoulder and addressed Wu. "You and I have a necromancer to see to."

"Quoi? I don't. I don't know what that is." Of course, she knew the woman meant the Ghost.

"Someone who augments his power through the dead."

Wu squinted, still feigning ignorance.

"A magus who kills others and uses their life force to fuel his spells, dear. Evil in its most base form." She searched in her bag and removed a thin string. Tightly pulling back her mound of gray curls, she bound the mass at the nape of her neck. "Only a necromancer can summon varrows to this plane." Her eyes twinkled with a challenge. "If you are afraid to face him, I understand. But you must point me in his direction so I can stop this."

Glancing over to the Tabari packing their caravan and then to the guards on the bridge, Wu felt torn. She had the Gbad spear. She could finally free Ekon as a leader of her tribe. Yet, the Racinian spoke one truth. The Ghost's evils must end.

When she turned back, the mage had already trod down the path Babhru had used to bring them here. Wu hurried to catch up. "I can take you to the date palm grove. From there, I will show you where to go."

They walked in silence at a slower pace than Wu was used to until they reached Najih's olive grove.

"What is your name, dear?"

Tersely, she answered, "Wu—Gbad'Wu."

"You do not care for me very much, do you, Gbad'Wu?"

She felt the woman's gaze on her. "You are Racinian."

"That makes rudeness acceptable?"

"My mother was Creb!" Wu snapped.

"Ah," Ailsa moaned. "An inherited bias, a learned hatred."

"Before Racine was an empire," Wu recited, "it was a large country. Before it was a large country, it was a small country tucked into the northeast border of Crebala. No bigger than a Warring State. Petite." Her mother's words trailed off in her memory. "Your kind take when it does not even appear you are doing so. It is in your blood. Your culture. In your habits. If someone notices or refuses your advances, they are crushed." Wu stopped. "Did you send Madhu to Trône d'Argent to save her or to give your Tower magics they never knew?"

Ailsa fixed her hands on her hips. "Now there's an accusation I do find offensive." She waved her hand in the air as though swatting away flies. "King Renauld or his son, King Clyde, is who you're angry with. Not me. It is time you cease those quarrels in your mind. They are long over."

"Pourquoi? Because there is no Crebala, it is done? For you, perhaps. I fight those quarrels every day!" She pointed her spear with her left hand back at Kruispad.

"It is because of them you even exist," Ailsa said. "Have you considered that?"

Wu stood silent.

Ailsa nodded. "While you think on it, Gbad'Wu, think on this: I agree with your opinion on the conflict—the conquest of Crebala. I see Racine's greed clearly, just as I see that light can come out of the dark." She gestured at Wu.

The mage grunted and carried on. "Bah. You call me Racinian, but I don't feel it. I wear the silver mantle, but I have not been in Racine since my son went to the Glades many, many years ago." She raised her hand up to the green streaks across the pale moon and let it fall. "Many scars ago. Do you know of the Glades?"

Wu sniffed. "It is as I said; my mother was Creb. I know of your old gods just as I know of the Daijon deities."

"Do you walk to the beat of their drums or follow your mother's faith?"

Wu rudely called Ailsa a fool with her squint. "I believe in good people. I believe in doing what is right. That is all that matters. Not your gods and their wants. If I am wrong, I invite them to tell me themselves." She threw her arms out and stared up to the heavens. "No?" She shrugged and carried on.

"What if they tell you in other ways?" Before Wu could respond, Ailsa waved off her own question and chuckled. "Ukresti would like you."

Considering the statement for a moment, Wu asked, "Which god is that?"

"She's no god, love, though some days . . ." Ailsa shook her head and rolled her eyes. "Ukresti leads my monastery, the Mount of Ukresti. Also, my employer. A stern woman, she is better at healing than humility."

"Quoi? You are a mage and a monk?" Her father's tales had often glorified monks. Stories of silent stalkers and unarmed warriors entertained the men of her tribe more nights than not. Wu never imagined one to look like Ailsa.

"I am a midwife for the order."

That made more sense.

Wu realized they had reached the edge of the date palm grove. She pointed southwest. "The satyr ruins are there, over that far dune. You will find the dead varrow in the woods first."

"Hmm." Ailsa studied the sandy terrain before them. "Well, if it must be, come along then."

Wu scoffed. "No. Did you not see what happened to Madhu? I am not going back there. Ekon needs me." She presented her spear and realized that meant nothing to the woman.

"You must come with me to the ruins."

"No. I said I would take you to the date palms and point you in the right direction. I have done as I said."

"Are you a little girl?" Ailsa asked. "Absorbed in her own world, her worries alone? If so, I have misjudged you." She frowned and shook her head. "That is not something I am prone to do. Does that spear not mean you lead your tribe, Daijon?" The mage smiled knowingly. "I can sense magic, you know?"

Ailsa walked on into the sand. "No, you must face him too. Come. I shall explain why this cold night must see his end. The reason has more to do with that red silk pouch in your belt than the dangers of one necromancer."

Wu's hand went to the pouch of beads at her side. "What does that mean?"

"Walk and talk," the Racinian commanded. "Isn't that what the Daijon do?"

As they went slowly across the sands, the woman requested Wu tell her what had taken them to the satyr ruins in the first place. The pieces Wu glazed over, like Ekon, Najih, and the Temple of Mulgrum, seemed to catch the woman's attention the most, pulling questions out of Ailsa more rapidly than a toddler. Finally, Wu agreed to divulge all, from meeting Madhu to stealing back her father's spear. Mangoes to varrows. Still, it did not sate the woman's hunger for knowledge.

"This is where we tied up Babhru," Wu said, pointing to the tamarind tree. "This is a tamarind tree." She pointed at her tracks. "This is where I carried Madhu. These are more trees."

"Yes, yes, very charming," Ailsa said tiredly. "If these are the woods, then we are close now?" When Wu nodded, Ailsa produced a small white linen pouch from her bag and dropped the sackcloth next to the tamarind tree. "Now, remember where I left this."

A forgetful mage. Bon. Wonderful. "Do you not need spells? Is that one enough?"

"Bah. I'm too old for that charade, love."

Wu didn't know what that meant but kept quiet until they reached the dead varrow. She heeled its broken ribs just for good measure.

"Ugly things, aren't they?"

"Have you fought these before?" Wu asked.

The old woman lamented in silence. "You too will see their kind again, Gbad'Wu. This evil drains Cyr. It is something my order aims to set right."

"You hunt varrows?"

"No," Ailsa said with a chuckle. She moaned as she settled onto a fallen tree to rest. "Well . . . I suppose you could say that I do hunt in a way. I find people who need to reconnect to the world. People who have been so hurt and have drifted so far into themselves and away from others that they can't see beyond the moment. Beyond the day. They can't see love, color, happiness beyond their memories of it. They survive. That is all." Her brown eyes roamed over Gbad'Wu with sympathy. "It is a sad occupation, but when I'm successful, there is no greater joy than bringing that soul back to the present."

"You cure them?"

"I wish I had such a gift." She laughed. "No. They must heal themselves, but the Mount helps. Ukresti helps." She studied the sky. "It'll be morning before we know it. We had best get this battle underway."

"Battle?"

"Mhmm. May my back hold out," Ailsa muttered. She rose and brushed off her seat. "Take me around the ruins to where this amphitheatre is, Gbad'Wu. Can we get there unseen?"

"I could," she answered frankly, eyeing the woman's hobble.

"Just pins and needles. It'll pass. Lead on."

"What will you do?" Wu asked. "Do you think you can kill him?"

The old woman's eyes grew sad. "We do not kill, Gbad'Wu. But there are times when death is the answer." She drew a deep breath. "I say we start with the manticore."

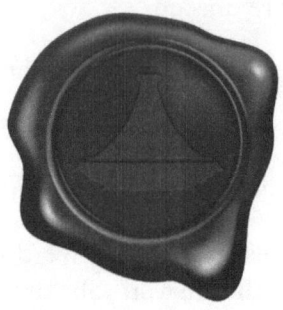

Chapter II: Hunted and Haunted

On their way around the northern end of the ruins to the amphitheatre, Gbad'Wu decided it best to give Ailsa a break. She crouched in concealment behind a tall stack of mattresses and spied through the slaver's tents, no longer littered with bodies to accompany the blood. The Ghost had posted four guards at the entrance to his underground lair. Their scimitars drawn, the men searched about at every breeze blowing the sand. She spotted another checking behind the marketplace's counters.

"And you do not know how many of them there are?" Ailsa whispered next to her.

"We were stealing, trying not to find his men," replied Gbad'Wu. "Why are we here, if you do not believe in killing?"

The mage considered her and settled to the ground on her hip. "Gbad'Wu, I must tell you something uncomfortable. Promise me you shall stay calm, for that is the only way we achieve success here."

Wu sank back to squat on her heels. "Je vous promets."

Watching the guards, Ailsa said, "There is a power we all possess. An energy. No matter what gods you believe in, that is true." Her gaze flitted to the bag of beads behind Gbad'Wu's belt. "Some necromancers have discovered a way to harness this energy and use it as they will. It makes them incredibly powerful but also traps the energy—the soul of the person they sacrifice."

"I do not understand," Wu said, though her stomach rolled.

"The bowl you found, the one set in the wall with the dark liquid . . ."

Gbad'Wu swallowed. "He called it his chalice." Slouching, she asked, "It was a head? There was a head in there?"

"Yes." She squeezed Gbad'Wu's forearm. "It wasn't the first." Again, her eyes fell to the gathered beads.

"You don't know that," Gbad'Wu said, ripping her arm free. But her mind had already begun fitting the pieces together. The blood staining the beads in the pit room, the beads of women. The Ghost had said he didn't want to see that liar's face. Her blinking quickened until she closed her eyes. Small and fragile, the hope her mother could still be found, that she had simply been sold off, vanished. Gbad'Wu tried to hold it in, but the best she could manage was to try to keep quiet when she recalled seeing Gbad'Zoya's beads as well.

"I am sorry, love," Ailsa said and rubbed Gbad'Wu's back. When Gbad'Wu's breathing slowed and she wiped her nose, the monk asked, "Do you understand what we're doing here?"

Gbad'Wu nodded. Through a tightened jaw, she said, "We are setting them free."

"Precisely. This is our purpose. To end the perversion of nature that is happening here."

Sneering at her thoughts, Gbad'Wu blurted, "You would let the Ghost live?" She flinched back from the finger thrown in her face.

"Bottle that," the old woman warned. She checked to make sure the guards hadn't heard. "Free your mother before you have thoughts of vengeance, you hear me? Your mother needs you with a clear mind and whole heart."

"Moi? You want me to go there in alone?"

"Calm yourself. The Ghost will be too busy with me to notice you." She slowly worked her way back into a crouch, more of a hunch really. "Shall we?"

When they left the tents, three more guards patrolled ahead of them. Wu kept a close watch for more until they reached the east end of the amphitheatre and discovered where the slavers' bodies had gone. She held Ailsa back until the men had circled around to the far side. "They will return soon."

Ailsa's breath caught.

Collared and entranced once more, the gray manticore stood in the center of the amphitheatre, surrounded by the men the Jomo tribe had defeated. Thick chains bound the beast's hind legs for good measure.

"Magnificent," Ailsa said. "And where is the pregnant one?"

Gbad'Wu frowned and shrugged. "This is the only one we saw." She stood in place as the monk edged nearer the manticore. Only when the mage stood at the beast's unmoving shoulder did Gbad'Wu dare follow, keeping an eye on its hovering stinger. Not as oblivious to the world around it as Wu had assumed, the manticore's ear twitched back at her approach.

Ailsa tapped her lip and studied the glowing script encircling the collar. "Her mate shall lead us to her." She reached for its neck.

Jutting her spear between the mage and the manticore, Wu said, "No! It will eat us!"

Ailsa threw Gbad'Wu a tired expression, pinched the spear, and lifted it out of her way. "They won't hunt unless both are freed. Manticore are very loyal to their mates." She pointed her chin to the manticore's hind feet. "We will pair the chaos of his escape with our own. Get the shackles off and hide somewhere. I'll remove the collar."

"He killed people earlier without her," Wu said.

Waving away the concern, Ailsa said, "The chains, please."

Even if Gbad'Wu had protested again, both metal cuffs sprang open. Worried, she watched the old woman and the beast as she ducked under its belly. Careful not to clink them against the stone, recalling what had happened to the elderly couple there hours earlier, Wu settled the heavy cuffs directly behind the manticore's massive paws.

After scurrying away from the mad woman and her plan, Wu scanned the area for guards and found shelter behind a fallen column between the amphitheatre and the ruined building where she and Madhu had spied.

Ailsa moved in front of the manticore and backed up several yards. She said something that Wu couldn't make out. The manticore's collar lost its glow, snapped apart, and crumbled. The monk mage lowered her hands and held the manticore's gaze as it roused.

The beast growled deeply and loudly enough to draw attention. Its tail arched up in a threat, dripping venom.

The mage raised a finger at it, scolding the beast.

It bared its fangs, then sniffed the air. It leaped up and spread its leathery gray wings. Flapping them several times, the manticore surveyed the grounds beneath it.

Guards shouted before Ailsa hurried to where Gbad'Wu hid and joined her.

"This is the wisdom of the monks that people revere?" Gbad'Wu asked, keeping an eye on the flying beast.

"Hush, now. Listen." Holding her finger up, the mage grinned when the manticore's roar came from the south. It sent a shiver up from Gbad'Wu's waist to her neck, but the mage appeared on the verge of laughter. "That shall keep them busy. Let's see if the entry is empty now. Then I shall occupy this Ghost while you destroy his 'chalice.'" She shuddered at the word.

"How am I to do this?" Gbad'Wu asked. "Break it?"

"Ah," the monk uttered. "A very important detail I nearly forgot." She opened her hand to reveal the tiny linen pouch she had been carrying. "Drop its contents inside the bowl to purify the water. When the water clears, it's done. Then you break the glass, and his pull on their souls shall end."

Peeking inside the pouch, Wu smelled citrus and apples from the mixture of seeds and petals. She closed it and nodded, less certain of her success than Ailsa.

"Now, let's get you inside."

They crept between the collapsing domed huts to the edge of the old marketplace. Two of the guards remained, staring south and bobbing up and down on their toes trying to see farther than they could.

"But did they tell their master?" Ailsa asked at a whisper. "Well, no matter. I shall draw him out. You sneak closer and get ready to run inside."

Tightening her grip on the pouch of seeds, Wu considered Ailsa's chances. "Are you sure you can stand against him?"

"That depends on how quickly you sever his link to those tortured souls. Go on now. Your mother needs you more than I do." The old woman formed a gentle cup shape with her hands and brought them together. A soft pink light swirled between them and formed a solid ball to hover between her hands.

"Merde," Gbad'Wu breathed.

"Language," Ailsa scolded. She clicked her tongue and tilted her head for Gbad'Wu to get going.

Taking advantage of the guards' distraction to the south, Gbad'Wu risked a direct route across the marketplace. She crept behind the counters of the thermopolia as she had with Madhu and, when certain she could easily make the last five yards to the entrance, rose up to nod at Ailsa.

Boldly, the elderly mage walked out into plain sight without detection from the distracted guards. The ball of pink light lifted with her hands above her head and swelled. As it grew, so did the light it cast, bringing an early dawn to the ruins.

That caught the guards' attention.

Ailsa flung her arms forward. The round boulder of light shot through the air and struck the worn tiles before the guards. Its impact hurled them back. The marketplace shook as the spell bored deeper, rumbling into the ground.

"I may have overdone that one," Ailsa said, conjuring two smaller orbs, one in each hand. She looked over to Wu and gestured her back. "Hide, girl. Only the fearless belong in this fight, those who have accepted their fates and their small place in this large world."

When Gbad'Wu had ducked down once more, Ailsa shouted, "I have come to see the man who believes himself above his brethren. Where is this Ghost? A man of wickedness? For I aim to smite him!"

A jolting boom shook the ruins again, sending up a cloud of dust.

Gbad'Wu wished the woman would hold back. She had to enter these ruins to save her mother after all.

Shouts rang out when the manticore's roar erupted again.

"Who dares?" the Ghost's voice blared.

Gbad'Wu cowered down against the counter from the unnaturally loud shout.

Rattling bones announced the Ghost's movement into the open.

"I dare," Ailsa yelled, "and I know better than to give you my name, you vile hobgoblin. So come, let us see if your stolen magics are any match for me. I am a mage of the Tower of Trône d'Argent and a monk of the Mount of Ukresti. Both would task me with bringing you low."

"Old woman," he said, amused, "your skin is not worthy of dusting my halls." Another rattle of the Ghost's bone jewelry got Gbad'Wu moving on her feet before the light of the moon dimmed. "If you seek the darkness, you have come to the proper place."

Risking a peek around the counter, Gbad'Wu saw the Ghost walking toward Ailsa. She paused, pondering if the halls below were vacant yet.

Ailsa hurled two balls of light at the necromancer. A dark shield blocked them, shattering one and sending the other crashing into the counter by Gbad'Wu.

Either way, she couldn't stay near this fight.

The Ghost laughed and raised his hands to the sky.

Gbad'Wu sprinted and leaped into the underground entrance just before purple bolts pelted the ground outside. She peeked out to see Ailsa shielded under her own magic. The woman already appeared to be flagging. She needed to hurry.

Running farther in, she reached the junction with the hall to the pits. Tapping and scraping made her turn. A horde of headless skeletons marched to aid their master.

"Oh no you don't," Wu said. She dashed ahead down the adjoining hall. She rounded the corner and slammed into a servant. Both jumped back.

"What—who are you?" the servant demanded.

She didn't have time for this. "You serve a wicked man," Gbad'Wu stated. Before the servant could finish his scoff, she smacked him with the butt of her spear. Her shoulder struck him hard beneath the ribs.

When he fell backward, his foot splashed into the green water of the cesspool. The man shrieked and flailed about as he wiped his foot on the mats lining the path.

"You are a traitor!" Wu yelled. "A traitor to all humankind. To life!" She raised her staff again.

But he shot to his feet and ran to one of the adjoining hallways. With a panicked glance back at her, he disappeared around the corner.

Fighting down her temptation to pursue him, she rounded the pool of sludge and cautiously breached the Ghost's treasure room. No one guarded it. Perhaps that was what his timid servant had been doing? Perhaps he believed himself invulnerable.

She went directly to the chalice and removed the gold lid, trying not to breathe or think about what was inside. She dumped the contents of the white linen pouch onto the sludge floating in the water and brought the pouch to her nose. The liquid inside the chalice sizzled, breaking down the clotted filth and thinning the water to clear as Ailsa had said it would.

When she reached up to replace the lid, something banged against the glass before her breasts. Gbad'Wu shrieked and fell back against the large trophy table, dropping the lid to clang against the tiles.

The head. It moved. Its flesh was swollen and loose. One glassy eye watched Gbad'Wu, tracking her movement. Its jaw worked, though she couldn't tell if it was trying to chew or speak. When the cleansing reached it, the head stilled. It fell aside and drifted to rest on the bottom of the glass.

The putrid air suddenly freshened with the smell of flowers. Hibiscus. "Maman?" Wu whispered. She glanced around the room. "Maman, is that you?"

A blast from above shook the lair, knocking books from the tables and glass vials to crash onto the floor. Ailsa needed her.

Gbad'Wu aimed the tip of her spear at the glass and punctured it with a quick strike. She stood away from the draining water and turned to go.

In the columned fountain chamber, women floated inches over the water. Too transparent to be real, the dozens of spirits appeared lost as they searched about. Gbad'Wu spotted a pale blue-and-purple necklace in the crowd and raced around the columns for a closer look with her hand over her heart. Wavy black hair. Fawn skin with rose undertones. A thin nose with a bump at the bridge. Beautiful green eyes.

"Maman . . . Maman!" Gbad'Wu shouted.

The spirit looked her way and smiled warmly. Her mother mouthed her name, but no sound came.

A hand lit on her mother's arm. Smiling as always, plump-cheeked Gbad'Zoya said something to her mother that Gbad'Wu could not hear. They both smiled her way before they put their hands on their hearts and pounded their fists twice to their chests. Her mother mouthed something that appeared to be, "So proud." Her image began to thin.

"Wait! Don't go!" Gbad'Wu nearly stepped into the water before she realized it had cleared as well. The olive-green water had concealed the answer to her unspoken question of what had happened to her mother's remains. The horror of so many heads, mostly skulls, forced her back. He had even added the head of Maris's statue to the depths.

Her mother waved her hand to get Gbad'Wu's attention. She put her finger under her chin and raised it.

Gbad'Wu nodded her understanding and stared into her maman's smile until it vanished. She wiped her nose on her forearm and knuckled away the tears from the corners of her eyes.

"You are free, Maman. Now I will make him pay."

Chapter 12: Nature's Course

Cutting the Ghost off from his reserves didn't soothe the battle above. Though the necromancer's lightning had gone and the moon's radiance returned to the marketplace, flashes from the forum still filled the corridor as Gbad'Wu raced to aid Ailsa.

Gbad'Wu peered out.

"Your games are over, hag," the Ghost yelled.

Forced back near the fence before the tents, Ailsa panted by the desecrated temple, bent over with her hands on her knees and her gaze stuck to the advancing necromancer. Blood darkened her robes down to her knee and splotched her gray shawl over her belly.

Scattered across the ground about Ailsa's feet, the Ghost's enslaved skeletons had returned to their rest. Her mother's bones among them. Gbad'Wu throttled her father's spear and prepared for a dash to end the Ghost once and for all.

"What you have taken from me," the Ghost said, "I can rebuild. Starting with your power." He raised both hands toward her.

Ailsa cried out.

Gbad'Wu raised her spear and stepped out to charge.

A blinding flash surrounded Ailsa. She disappeared.

Blinking away the blue splotch centered in her vision, Gbad'Wu retreated back.

"Now you hide?" the Ghost roared. "You insult me by wasting my time, woman. As a wight, I will make you dance for my customers until your flesh has all fallen from your bones." His bone bracelets clacked, teasing Ailsa with his threat.

As her sight cleared, Wu noticed the downed guards by the lair's entrance. Their bodies had been drained; their skin had shriveled and dried to reveal the bones within. Ailsa's spell hadn't done that. She wouldn't kill. A pang of guilt altered Wu's plan. Perhaps it was seeing her mother again. Perhaps it was knowing what Ailsa had given her. But if this plan worked, which it probably wouldn't, she would uphold Ailsa's principles. If not, well, so be it. The Ghost must be slain.

Gbad'Wu snuck a peek. The Ghost searched Maris's Temple from the stairs. Creeping forward, she eased the desiccated man's long scimitar from his belt.

"Come out, witch!" the Ghost yelled. It echoed back at him from within the temple.

Calming her breathing, Gbad'Wu crouched out in the open and readied herself as she snuck forward a few yards more. Her senses sharp and her pulse wild, she sprang into a run. Held out to her side, the tip of the scimitar clinked against the stone counters in her dash, then it fell to scrape the tiles of the ancient marketplace, bouncing along in her direct dash at the Ghost.

Spotting her, the Ghost laughed. He bent over guffawing. "Is this the spirit sent to deliver my punishment? One little girl?" His fingers curled as he straightened. His long fingernails danced before his grinning white face. "The girl who stole my spear."

He broiled the air around her but not quickly enough to catch her. She threw the scimitar to clatter across the ground to his feet.

The Ghost snarled and kicked the blade away. He splayed his fingers at her as heat rushed in at her sides.

She leaped forward and rolled. Wu raised her spear and charged at him with a yell, emptying her lungs.

Three long darts struck the Ghost's chest, stopping her cold.

The slim venomous quills worked quickly, stiffening his muscles. He fell forward, his wrist catching him on the stairs. Though his bones snapped, he never broke his pose.

A whoosh overhead caused Wu to hunch. Landing on the temple stairs, a mane-less gray manticore set a possessive paw on the Ghost and stared Wu down. Her barbed tail whipped behind her, warning Wu back.

Her free hand raised, Wu backed away slowly.

The manticore bit into the Ghost's side and issued a satisfied growl.

Wu backed away farther, unable to break her watch of the beast enjoying her own vengeance, warranted and visceral. When she reached the wall opposite the forum, the male arrived. As they nuzzled and shared the kill, Wu slipped into the building.

Whatever it had once been, this building displayed the frescos she had expected from the satyrs, perhaps less crude.

"Wu," a voice called weakly. "Gbad'Wu."

Following Ailsa's call, she came to an atrium where frescoed fauns played with fairies and wolves. She found Ailsa flat on her back atop a patch of grass and pale yellow wildflowers watered by a broken ewer-shaped fountain slowly burbling on the wall. Her hands lay over her chest and barely rose with her breath. The blood of her injuries had soaked the left side of her shawl now.

Ailsa's eyes opened at her approach. "I saw the manticore," she said, glancing up to the orange-tinged sky above the atrium. Only then had Gbad'Wu realized the sun had started to rise. "Did it find its master?"

Gbad'Wu grinned slightly and nodded. Then she inhaled deeply. "I thank you for saving my friend. My maman. All of those women. Merci, Ailsa. You were not the corrupted Racinian I thought. I am sorry for treating you that way."

An uncertain groan came from the ailing woman. "There is something I must confess too. You were . . . somewhat right about the Racinian silver in my blood, Gbad'Wu. The Tower of Trône d'Argent may gain great knowledge from Madhu and Raza, as I intended." She raised an eyebrow. "And Madhu may learn some much needed discipline."

Gbad'Wu had to laugh at that. She put her hand over Ailsa's.

"I'm sorry I sent your friend away, dear." Ailsa coughed and winced. "Forgive me."

"I can. But Madhu may not."

Ailsa rolled her eyes. "That girl is the type who makes the best of every situation. I only wish I could witness Sylvester's inevitable and perpetual frustration." Her features softened as she met Gbad'Wu's gaze. "Did you get to see your mother, love?"

The question pricked at the mounting emotions of the evening. Weeping, Wu nodded.

"Isn't that something?" The old woman smiled. "I'd guess your father is at rest too, knowing she's safe and you lead his tribe."

Not bothering to clear her face of the dampness, Gbad'Wu nodded and said, "I will bury them all." The task ahead felt monumental. She'd never be able to discern whose bones were whose.

"Why?" Ailsa asked.

The question surprised Gbad'Wu.

"They are at rest." Ailsa wiped away Wu's tears before settling her hand back on her chest. "No. Your parents and I give you permission to forget this cursed place, Gbad'Wu. There is nothing here but history, and you are the type who creates it, young lady. Don't you want to see the world? The Tabari are only one race, one culture you have experienced. Look at what you have learned from them, how much stronger you are. There are many more peoples out there waiting to be discovered. Learn from them. Heal yourself. And heal Cyr."

Gbad'Wu understood what she was saying. A final attempt to recruit for her monastery. But, in truth, what options did she have? The Jomo tribe would welcome her and Ekon, but their wounds were just as grievous and tied to this place. Elsewhere . . . elsewhere sounded refreshingly new. Hopeful.

"Good girl," Ailsa rasped. She cleared her throat. "Take my bag. In it, there is a map to the Mount. Use it. Get your Ekon, use that spear of yours, and get yourself to Ukresti. She'll do right by you."

"Gbad'Ekon," Wu corrected with a small smile.

Ailsa's wizened eyes searched Wu's face before she smiled. "I believe in you. Now you must go, dear. The manticore will finish with that bony man soon enough and return to their hunt. I only pray I may sate their appetite long enough for your return to Kruispad."

Gbad'Wu started to protest, but the woman said, "Go! I'll be gone from this world before you reach the woods."

Instead, Gbad'Wu remained kneeling at Ailsa's side and sang the lullaby her mother had repeated to her until she slept as a child. She repeated it once more after Ailsa had stopped breathing.

As she got up to go, she noticed a shimmer beneath Ailsa's shawl. Gbad'Wu gently unfolded the wool to find a Daijon necklace in gray beads. She read the necklace aloud. "Our roots all touch."

Sneaking past the manticore wasn't difficult. They lounged and napped on the stairs of the temple in the warming sun. Still, Gbad'Wu ran all the way to the woods and the shelter of the trees. Before she went too far, she looked back to the satyr ruins. "Merci, Ailsa. Maman, Papan . . . je vous aime."

Chapter 13: The Gbad Tribe

Ailsa's words played through Wu's mind again as she walked the road to Kruispad under the sunrise. "We do not kill." Then how exactly could she free Gbad'Ekon from Najih? The man deserved it. He deserved worse. Worse was probably acceptable to Ailsa's beliefs. Gbad'Wu let that thought carry her back to Kruispad. Her daydreams enthralled her so deeply she didn't snap out of them until she stood at the gate to Najih's estate.

Antomé's face paled upon seeing her spear. His hand slowly reached for the gold-sheathed short sword at his hip.

Gbad'Wu stood her spear on its end and raised her hand to stall him. "I am Gbad'Wu. One of my tribe is being held here." She reset her hand on her spear. "You have been kind to me. I urge you not to lose your life in protection of the monster inside those walls."

He set his jaw and drew his short sword. "It is my reputation that feeds my livelihood, little one."

"S'il vous plaît," she pleaded, tilting the shaft of her spear, ready to counter a strike. "It is your soul that suffers. I have seen it in your eyes. Do not let this place, this man, do to you as he has done to so many of us."

Antomé laughed. "You misunderstand me. Najih Gorondo is filth. But I must eat." He nodded to the gate and swung it open. Baskets still lined the wall to the right. The others had yet to leave the shack. "You must make it look as though you took me by surprise. Then I saw no one." He shrugged and winked.

She directed him to step back farther behind the gate, where he would not be discovered by accident. "I take no pleasure from striking you, Antomé." The white flash of his genuine smile stalled her swing, but freeing Gbad'Ekon was her responsibility. "I am sorry for this pain." Regardless, she swung the black steel butt of the spear with enough force to knock him flat and grimaced at her success. "That is what you get for smiling too much," she said. "Now, I must move quickly before someone finds you."

Through Najih's kitchens, she crept. No one noticed her, too busy with their early morning chores to watch the walls. Or the stairs. Up, she went.

Lacquered and gilded furniture filled the passageways and sitting rooms on the way to his private bedchamber.

In a sea of embroidered pillows and silk blankets, Najih slept on his round bed in the center of the room. Ornamented for him even in sleep, Gbad'Ekon had curled away as far from his reach as possible. The man's arm lay stretched out, his fingers inches from the small of her back.

Gbad'Wu moved to her friend's side and held her spear over her, the tip of the point hovering before the man's gut. She pricked him.

Najih cried out. His yellowing brown eyes bulged.

Gbad'Ekon jerked awake and flinched when she saw the spear over her.

"I am not a flea. I am Gbad'Wu, the leader of the Gbad tribe."

The man shuffled away from beneath his sheets, his mouth hanging open. His hand went to the spot of blood on his blue silk robe. "You dare!

Your tribe died at the hands of that mad Dokka Roho. You have no one and no protections for what you are doing here."

Wu lowered her chin. "You knew his name?" Her hold on fury lessened.

Gbad'Ekon slid out of bed and stood beside her. "She has me. Gbad'Ekon."

Retracting from them, Najih asked, "You?" He laughed. "You are mine!"

When he reached for her, Gbad'Wu swung her spear tip up to float before his neck. "Gbad'Ekon is stronger than me. She will not stay on your lead. The sheikh's law states you must show respect and hospitality to the Daijon tribes. That means us. Let us leave without pursuit, and we will forgive the trespasses you have put upon us here." She glanced over to Gbad'Ekon, aware it wasn't truly her trespasses that held the most weight.

Gbad'Ekon's pink nails lit on Gbad'Wu's shoulder when she nodded.

"The sheikh?" Najih asked. "Little girl, I am friends with the sheikh."

Wu suddenly felt weak. The tip of the spear fluttered. They'd never make it to the border if Najih had the royal guard tracking them.

"He lies," Gbad'Ekon said flatly, adding her strength to holding the spear steady. She threw a challenging expression across the bed. "He says this a lot about the sheikh, but I have never seen proof of such a kinship."

"You dare! You are my wife, and you will stay!" he yelled. "You belong to me. The law says you are my property!"

"No," Gbad'Ekon said coolly, "I do not belong to you, Najih." She released the spear and removed the ruby ring from her marriage finger. She flung it at him. "This belongs to you." She unclasped the diamond-studded collar around her neck. "This does." She tossed it onto the bed. In two swift motions, she brushed away her thin golden bracelets into clattering heaps on the blankets. "These do." She didn't stop at the jewelry. As she untied the knot at her side holding her robes closed, she said, "These silks are yours. But I never gave myself to you willingly. I am not and could never be yours no matter what your laws say."

As he thought, Najih's nostrils twitched. He huffed through his bottom teeth as his lip hung open. "You will go naked?" He barked a laugh and loomed forward darkly. "I will let them kill you on the charge of indecency."

"If it is the price to be free of you, so be it."

He reached to smack her, but the ever-keen edge of the Gbad spear nicked his neck. His anger redirected itself down the weapon as he swatted the splotch of blood on his skin. "Stupid girls. You will die before you reach Hibadago! The desert will claim you!"

"Then we will die," Gbad'Wu said.

"Yes," Ekon agreed. "A thousand times, yes."

Cautious of Najih's reach, Gbad'Wu rounded the bed with her spear poised. When they had backed up to the doorway, she fled with Gbad'Ekon to the stairwell.

She heard the whispering silks of Najih's robes shuffling after them and turned.

"You are mine!" He grabbed Gbad'Ekon's arm.

Gbad'Ekon snatched the jeweled hairpin from her hair.

"No!" Gbad'Wu yelled.

But it was too late. Red spread out from the hairpin's prongs lodged in old man's heart. For a few seconds, Najih stared in wonder at it, then at Gbad'Ekon. He collapsed.

Gbad'Ekon bent down. "You never owned me or any of us." She pulled the hairpin free and stood over the man while his blood seeped out.

As she watched Najih's death, Gbad'Wu wondered what this meant. What would it do to Gbad'Ekon? Ailsa ultimately gave her life to avoid taking another herself. But why? Without thinking, she said, "We are going somewhere that can help."

"Where?" Ekon tilted her head. "How did you get the spear back?"

"Get dressed, Gbad'Ekon. Accusations of murder will be chasing us now. We don't want extra attention."

While Ekon readied herself and packed extra clothes and jewels to barter, Gbad'Wu watched the stairs for anyone who may happen upon Najih's body. She wasn't sure how to explain what they would see or what actions she would be forced to take to protect herself and Ekon.

Thankfully, no one came before Gbad'Ekon returned in pale blue. Racinian blue. Gbad'Wu said nothing for the color or the bloody pin still clutched in her hand.

Gbad'Ekon brought her away from Najih and down the stairs. Through the kitchens and the side passage, they crept and found the sunlight.

"Wait," Gbad'Wu said when Ekon started for the gate. Casually holding the spear at her side, Gbad'Wu went to where the orphans were gathering their baskets for their day's work.

A few of the children cried out in fear upon seeing her. Gbad'Wu put up her hand and then put her finger to her lips. When they listened, she said, "Najih is dead. You may stay here and be placed with another master by the temple. Or you may join the Gbad tribe and journey with us to the Mount of Ukresti. There, we will be welcomed, sheltered, and educated."

Little Arun ran to Gbad'Wu's side. The others shifted on their feet and searched each other's faces for what to do.

A hand seized Gbad'Wu's spear. She slapped her other hand to it and pulled it back from Rouzbeh.

He was stronger. Struggling to keep both of her hands on it, she lifted slightly from the ground. "I will lead you," he said to the others. "And we won't take these nasty trespassers."

Gbad'Wu scraped her sandal down his bare shin and slammed her forehead into his face. It hurt. But the blood draining from his nose made her smile. She settled into a warrior's stance with the tip of the spear aimed at his heart. "Come forward," she said.

Undeterred, Rouzbeh sneered and came at her.

A hollow clang rang out. Rouzbeh fell forward. If Gbad'Wu hadn't been quick, he would have impaled himself.

Kahlil frowned at the small black cauldron in his hand, still sticky with gruel. "I will not go with you," he said quietly. "But I am sorry for what I did to you." His brown face wore genuine remorse.

Gbad'Wu stood up straight and forgave him with a nod.

"Give us the hairpin," Kahlil said to Gbad'Ekon. "Those of us who stay . . ." He looked over the orphans, extending his own offer. "We will tell the city guard we found Rouzbeh with it." He kicked Rouzbeh. "We don't know what happened to Ekon."

"Merci," Gbad'Ekon said. She glanced down at the bloody pin her hand, then handed it over.

"Merci," Gbad'Wu repeated. Recalling Raza's words, she added, "My tribe is eternally grateful for your kindness, Kahlil."

Kahlil nodded. "I will get the guard."

Slamming the spear's steel end on the ground, Wu regained the orphans' attention and silenced the hubbub. "It is a long way to the Mount. I know how tired we all are, but I ask of you to consider this. If you stay, nothing changes for you. If you go with us . . ." She smiled at Ekon. "Everything may change." Without waiting for confirmation from any of them, she led the way past Antomé, through the gate, and out of Kruispad. The ancient highway was an odd choice for a Daijon tribe, but they would need to barter for supplies along the way. Hunting would only slow them.

When Kruispad was a small town on the horizon, Gbad'Wu finally checked to see who had followed. Fourteen, beyond Ekon and Arun. Some had taken their staffs and baskets. Many had wrapped themselves in their blankets. One had taken Antomé's sword. Though she felt a little guilty about that theft, she smiled and slowed to welcome each to the Gbad tribe.

Arun took Gbad'Wu's left hand when they continued their march. "Am I Gbad'Arun now?" he asked.

Gbad'Wu smiled down at him. "You are whoever you want to be. That is what it means to be free, mon petit chou."

Chapter 14: Ukresti

Winter had begun in most of the known world, but it had hardly touched the jungles at the southern end of the Asdales Mountain Range. Thankfully, the higher Gbad'Wu and her tribe climbed, the less humid and unforgiving the weather became. The steep climb winded her. Her body ached from her heels up to her shoulders. Her lungs drank in the muggy air yet were never satisfied. She sank down to sit on the stone steps that, according to a local pale-skinned Dessrini tribe, would bring them to Ukresti. "Another break," she said to her followers.

Tired and hungry, they drooped to the stones.

"Wu," Gbad'Ekon said. She nodded up the stairs.

Another fifty steps up, the climb ended at a pair of tall solid teak doors inset into a rounded gray-stone tower capped with a cone of red-slate shingles.

"Wait here," Gbad'Wu said to the others. With a breath, she set her

102

determination and climbed.

A short distance up, the dense vegetation ceased on her left with the drooping mountainside, allowing her a view of the lush valley. Large white birds soared below her, so far below she saw only specks, not unlike what she had seen in the forest's high canopy as they had passed beneath it yesterday.

The final eight steps to the Mount were wooden and suspended over a torrent of gushing water. Gbad'Wu tested the weathered bridge with a few solid taps from her spear before continuing up to try the door.

Entering the tower's darkness, Gbad'Wu heard water falling deep within. Her eyes took a moment to adjust and permit her to see a wide passage continuing into the mountainside.

In the shadows of the passageway, a figure watched her back. The woman approached with confidence and, in her creaseless eyes, caution. Red scales interrupted her wheat-colored skin in patches and gloved both arms from her elbows to her fingertips. A mirokar? As she circled Gbad'Wu wordlessly, her long black fingernail tucked a braid of her short dark hair over her ear.

Realizing she was staring rudely at the taller woman, Gbad'Wu turned her eyes to the floor and said, "Ailsa—"

Faster than Gbad'Wu could follow, the woman attacked. She slammed her ankle into the back of Gbad'Wu's knee and shoved her. Gbad'Wu fell hard to the flagstones. She rose to her elbows, angry then broiling. The point of her father's spear held her down, looming above her breast.

Rolling the shaft in her fingers, the woman frowned and studied the weapon.

She said something Gbad'Wu didn't understand. Whether it was the accent overlaying her Common or the mirokar's forked tongue, Gbad'Wu wasn't sure. "What?"

Crisply, the mirokar repeated, "Who are you?"

Gbad'Wu leaned forward and put the tip of her father's spear to her throat. "I am the one Ailsa Briggs sent to find you. I am the one who has led my tribe across the deserts and through the jungle to train with Ukresti. I am Gbad'Wu! That is my spear. Who are you? If not Ukresti, do not test my patience."

"Explain."

Scowling, Gbad'Wu said, "This truly is where Ailsa trained." Still, she tersely relayed her tale of the Ghost, Madhu, and their journey to find the Mount of Ukresti. When she finished, her temper had waned some. Revisiting the events calmed her, as remembering her mother's smile and Madhu often did.

The woman withdrew the spear and leaned against it. "You have traveled far, even for a Daijon. How could I refuse such commitment?" She dropped the black steel end of the spear to the floor next to Gbad'Wu's hand and waited for her to take it. At the door, the mirokar called down to the others. "Come. Come, Gbad tribe. I am Ukresti. You are welcome here at my Mount."

Gbad'Wu rose and wore encouragement for her tribe as they entered, all the while not meeting Ukresti's stare and hoping she hadn't made a terrible mistake.

The mirokar's red-scaled hand lit on Ekon's shoulder as she passed. "Gbad'Ekon?" she asked.

When Ekon glanced to Gbad'Wu, she came forward.

"I will take that as a 'yes,'" Ukresti said. "Now that this Najih is dead, are you free of him?"

Gbad'Ekon looked to her hands, then crossed her arms over her breasts. "No. I see him . . . in my mind. All the time."

The mirokar nodded and tilted her head forward to whisper, "We will make him go away." Abruptly, she walked to the passageway. "Come. Cyr herself welcomes you. Here at the Mount of Ukresti, you will find food and shelter, as well as discipline and purpose."

Gbad'Wu adopted her encouragement again for Gbad'Ekon and the others.

Ekon ushered in Arun and the rest of their tribe.

When they had all entered the chamber with the waterfalls beyond the passageway and Ukresti had begun escorting the group farther in, Gbad'Wu reopened the grand doors to the monastery and stepped outside into an afternoon shower. After she had taken a few steps down the wet stone stairs, the door creaked opened again.

"Come rest," Ukresti said from the doorway. "You have traveled far in land and in life to get here, Gbad'Wu. It is deserved."

Continuing down, Gbad'Wu said, "I cannot. Not yet."

"How many did you lose?"

Gbad'Wu halted and turned to face Ukresti.

The mirokar tilted her head and nodded for Gbad'Wu to come inside.

"Three," Gbad'Wu answered. "In the fog that rolled in the morning before last." She stepped down again. "I must go."

"The Cloud is no fog," the mirokar stated. "Tell me, what did you hear?"

Gbad'Wu closed her eyes and lowered her chin. The guttural noises she had hoped the children had not heard played through her mind. She had wanted to believe the absence of screams meant the others had been taken alive. That they could be saved. "They are my tribe."

"You would not even recognize their remains."

Gbad'Wu glared up at her.

The mirokar flung the monastery door open wider. "But there are countless others you could save." This time Ukresti let the door slam itself closed.

Enjoying the isolation for a moment, Gbad'Wu sat and mourned the three lost members of her tribe. With training, she would fail less. She refused to lose more.

With a long glance out over the treetops, she made an unspoken promise to her parents to uphold their traditions when possible and to honor those who came before them, those now lost. She double-tapped her fist to the blue-and-purple beaded necklace carrying her father's message of love for her mother.

Gbad'Wu ascended.

THANK YOU FOR READING!

IF YOU ENJOYED *THE GHOST IN THE DUNES*, PLEASE WRITE A REVIEW. YOUR ENCOURAGING WORDS BRIGHTEN MY DAY AND INSPIRE ME TO CONTINUE SHARING MORE TALES FROM CYR.

Other Books in the Lamentation's End series:

About the Author

Wade Lewellyn-Hughes is an author, screenwriter, and general creative based in Montana. Aiming to bring a vivid world and robust characters to life, he values diversity and differences in this world and the one he's writing.

Sign up for updates on upcoming books and find out more here: http://wadelewellyn.com